The Old Man and the Sazerac

Malic Laneaux

TABLE OF CONTENTS

Dedication:

For those who view the world with more than just eyes; for those who feel the gem inside.

Chapter 1: Is this the end?

Is this the end? The fall of intimacy, this crumble of curiosity? Oh, how frail compassion becomes in the hands of two lovers; through their words, movements, and actions. And still, this becomes an infatuation at its reach—a ticking time bomb of youth versus love, of chaos compared to calm. Here we have a lust too lunacy seeming so sporadic, yet there is some cause for blame; some reason for the end of that spark—a spark that now appears to subside. But there was a moment when at first sight created flames of passion and fire, a fire that now seems so far gone ever ember has lost its power. All of the oxygen, a sad memory, the warmth, a past reflection, and as our relationship falls apart onto the floor, neither one feels able to retrieve such heavy pieces. As this collective sense of disquietude engulfs the entire apartment, I can not help but ponder; Am I truly to blame?

Thoughts take me as two sapphires glossed with hurt and frustration look over at me. Her pain is evident; pain caused by the witless actions of a youth searching, lost, and uncomfortable. Still, as I look at her, each sapphire is so beautiful, so blue, even with tears. There is a light that comes trapped within their glimmer, a flicker of Eden—a reflection, and still so much more lurks deep within each iris.

Sorrow has developed into anger and confusion, creating this dense elixir that threatens to alter our relationship. Where love once lived, contempt now lingers, and I can't help but feel this might be all she can handle. All of the arguments, the fuck ups, all of the constant disappointments. This might be the end, an erosion of enchantment slipping through my doltish fingertips.

Unintentionally I have caused a strain that destroys her beauty. Unintentionally I have created stress that clouds the sapphire of her eyes. Unintentionally I have turned love into anguish, and I have no idea what to do. Is this the stress and strain of a fool's coupling? Am I to blame for vacant beauty, the evaporation of essences, of love? Thoughts skates past mind as Illegra prepares for her verbal assault.

"Do you even fucking care?"

Her tone is like a dagger, slicing the air between us. Assuredly, Illegra has been sharpening her most dangerous weapon with social media posts, finding girls' numbers on my phone, and the usual stories about my city-wide antics. With that in mind, I fight back the chance to speak, detaining words out of fear or machismo; I can't entirely be sure.

Illegra looks to me, yet no answer follows. No dribble from my lips, not even a gasp or deep breath, no pushed air from my nostrils, just quiet or as slow as an apartment complex can be. She stares into me as I stand with farce stoicism, as though fools survive with pride.

"You know, you really are a piece of shit, and everyone told me. They warned me about big bad Malic."

Illegra's tilted head is condescending, provoking even; mannerisms that promote the full extent of her chagrin and a look on her face that would scare any dictator. But it is her emphasis on "everyone told me," which holds a long sting, taunting me with "big bad" as though I were a joke. It makes me wonder, boils me up, I begin feeling slight insecurities, pride momentarily shattered. Everyone? Who could be everyone? Still, Illegra continues, with each word of her thick east coast accent pounding away at any sense I might have. Harsh words echo throughout the apartment, words that ripple on the sea of my doltish emotions, my pride. Thick clouds of aggravation mixed with confusion float through the air, this miasma of misfortune; it is a stench that takes all of me to ignore.

In these moments, with the apartment at high anxiety, Illegra flustered; the tension makes me feel mad—crazy like I could lose my mind. I feel cornered—frightened. I can feel the confrontation, and I don't much like confrontation. Confrontations often set off every fight or flight preceptor in my brain—with flight seeming the best option. I would prefer an escape from this argument then stand around for a verbal lashing. That's my road. A fool's exit seems imminent; best grab my Jay's, call the boys, and hit the "Rum."

I look over to a pair of shoes, then quickly glance at Illegra, averting the magnetism of sapphire. I close my lids while allowing her words to fill the room. My gorgeous Illegra's stunning features have taken a back seat to grief and turmoil, showing a vivid reflection of our coupling; I try not to look. Our disquietude, her indignation, which is my current creation continues; assault after assault, an assortment of discomforts and shortcomings, name-calling, the whole gamut of male-bashing. A verbal lashing so cruel and honest I can't help but bleed my lip. Illegra intends to let me have it, to speak her mind, clear the air, but my onyx and sense will not be captured.

Looking at "Leggy" when she is being irrational pains me; it sucks my infatuation away. Even a rational Illegra could put fear into any man whilst maintaining the attraction, the piercing gaze, and sharp words, but I cannot bear seeing her like this. As the heat of each word ignites from her lips, I feel as though hell could rise. With more than our relationship hanging in the balance, there is danger. I better get out of here. I must leave before Illegra creates scars that won't mend—scars that will take her words from this brief spat into a complete fallout. What a disenchantment of something that was once so beautiful. I must get out of here. Why wait around to get verbally abused? I don't need this. It is time to grab my things and make a hasty retreat. This is getting out of hand; it's…

"Malic."

My name in her mouth chills the fire for a split second. It is soft and welcoming; I ignore it.

"Malic!"

Illegra shouts, attempting to raise some emotion—to boil me up, but her words fall to unwitting ears. Her tone threatens that this might be the last time she is willing to raise her voice—the last time she is willing to fight for me—the last time sapphire meets onyx with the warmth of love, that intimate, pure, pure love. Illegra is reaching out to me, yet I must

refuse. I have already come to terms with my retreat; there is nothing left that she can say or do. Youth be damned, for you are now in control.

"Ugh," her gasp fills the room, bouncing off every wall, reverberating a newfound resentment. No more whimpers, her tears subside, with each alabaster hand finding a home on each hip. If I were to look at her now, I might turn to stone or die. Forcing the onyx to my feet, I look away, down to my black And1 socks. This is the first step in my withdrawal from her; the white flag of my surrender is cast. Illegra can feel the rejection, the energy between us, the nothingness. I look to my feet like a whipped dog, defeated, desperate to escape this moment.

"You are a fucking coward. A worthless, pointless, spineless, fucking coward."

Verbal daggers fly through the air, impaling my pride with the word "coward." She states it all so decisively that her voice need not raise one decibel. It was a whisper, if not a scream. A slap of silk more brutal than any words I have heard in recent history. Illegra's comments continue cutting deep, eyes lasers of disappointment, these sapphire beams I am desperate to escape. As she begins walking over to me, the broiling of aggravation steams the space between us. From nothingness to heat and the seasons bear no guilt in this thick slice of tension. Hell does not freeze over; it engulfs the land.

"You're just going to run away, aren't you?… Just run away, as you always fucking do. Like the beaten little dog that knows no better."

The subtle nuances of her accent buzz in each ear, strong, direct, and with no honey. Her words, that look, this heat, all aimed to hurt my pride, to invoke emotion and desire. Still, I save face. Illegra's smacking lips and eye rolls hope to demean my self-esteem; each look, each wave of her hand, the hot breath, all meant to create a rise out of me, a reaction; meant to bait me into this fight or any fight. Yet still, without a flench, I stand. Even after being called a coward, I stand uninvolved and unbothered even while she points her fingertips into my chest; I stand.

Who needs this? What's the point? Why do women love to argue and nag so damn much? These hand waves in my face, the snapping of her fingers, it's all so vexing, so unattractive. Actions such as these only reiterate that the single life suits me best. That being the man I am and in this city, I don't need this. Who needs this? Who in their right mind would deal with this? Enough is enough; time to get out of here.

"Of course, I'm leaving—I need air. Whenever you get like this, I just ...."

The words bust out of my mouth as I create space with my aggressive hand movements. Then, Illegra had me cornered in this living room; now, my words break that hold.

"Whenever I get like what?"

Illegra snaps back with animated hands more frantic than my own. Her first push is light fairing, but her next push is nothing to sneeze at, almost knocking me back into the coffee table. My sharp look warns Illegra of the danger, but the Italian flames have taken her over. She steps closer, her voice raises.

"You mean whenever I confront you on your bullshit? Whenever I catch you in some shitty lie?"

Illegra's disgust is as apparent as the shake of her head, and that look, that confused, unattractive look, a look making me yearn for an exit, the bar, my boys, makes me want to leave this entire situation. Is this truly what we have become? That shitty arguing couple.

"Oh my God! You are such a fucking COWARD! You always become such a fucking coward when I catch you in some bullshit. You make me look like a fucking fool with all of this childish bullshit. Grow the fuck up, Malic!"

Illegra's head shake proves this might be the end; the stream flowing sapphire to lip might be that final sign, the last reach, and her words hope to tear me apart. We stare deep into each other. Her sapphire meets my onyx, waiting for retort, warmth, or any sign that I care. Illegra is reaching out to me, with a look, with her energy, this heat, even with her disparaging words. In her funny way of keeping me interested and showing her love, she has become this unattractive, emotionally chaotic bully.

I will give it to her; she knows how to push my fucking buttons, and there is nothing more aggravating than her standing right here, in my way, right under my skin. These emasculating pushes and name-calling, the looks she gives, her highs, her lows, it's all so dramatic. It's drama; and Illegra knows I hate drama. Yet, none of that compares to the anger I feel when being labeled a coward. Nothing, and I mean nothing, infuriates me more than that fucking word, and Illegra, of all people, knows that.

"What bullshit? Anytime I'm not home or give you what you call "enough attention," you accuse me of cheating. Whenever I want to hang with the boys or play some ball, you assume I'm with another woman; you assume I'm trying to get away with something. You are always looking for the worst. So I ask you, what do you want from me? When does this attention hoarding nonsense end?"

The height of my voice knocks Illegra down to size as sapphires become sea. My conviction and harsh rhetorical questions are the only comforts left near the couch as I walk past her, searching for better shoes. I move past, put off by what has transpired. I do not push past, as I would never put my hands on a woman, but my movement is aggressive, sporadic, forcing Illegra to step aside. Walking down the hallway, I avoid seeing pictures and memories; I avoid looking at anything that might urge me to stay. Once in our room, I immediately spot the jays I will wear. I grab my shoes, take a seat at her vanity, then prepare for my exit. Of course, Illegra follows behind, adding proper percussion to the orchestra of our divide. Assuredly our neighbors will not be listed among fans of this dramatic theater. Ignoring her trample, I start with my left shoe, avoiding her gaze as I tie. Yet still, I feel her; there is still something there; I feel those sapphires reaching out to me, hoping to pull me in, wanting me, needing me.

"I just want to spend time with you."

Illegra grabs me by the chin, gently forcing onyx to sapphire. Her hands are warm; they feel like home. Still, something keeps me away; something in me screams "leave."

"Every time you leave, every time you are out at a bar or with the fucking "boys," it's as if I don't matter. It's a sign that you don't care."

I pull my face away from her hand, then grab my other shoe. The truth of what she says stings, but the youth of my mind does a fine job of avoiding the spice. Illegra is reaching out while my youth pulls me away. I do not need this; I don't want to be in this apartment listening to her meandrous yearn for something my youth will not allow.

"All I want to know is if I'm your girl or not. I just want to know that I matter. I need to know if this feeling in my gut is…."

The final words come out softly, but the gravity of her statement reverberates throughout the entire apartment—throughout my entire foolish body. She stands by the chair in silence, sapphire lost and dripping. I sit holding my right shoe in hand in the absence of words, but I'm not sure I would speak even if I had them.

"Most don't even know that I'm your girl. Hell, I don't even know if I'm your girl."

The apartment stays silent for a moment; no appliances blaring, no clocks ticking, just the echo of Illegra's honest words. Manic is the heart of mine, which pounds almost out of control. I take a deep breath and exhale that breath whilst holding the most stoic of features manageable.

"Am I your girl?"

The sincere sadness and confusion lodged in her throat, reaching out to me, hoping to grasp my love. What an intimate interrogation, one that should be so simple yet is not. Like a puzzle missing that most crucial piece, her love does not fit the missing parts of this picture. Is love what completes the coupling or what divides it? Is it possible that the moment you fall into love, you slowly begin to fall out?

"Don't you understand that I love you?"

Illegra falls to her knees right between my legs as I fidget with my right shoe.

"I feel like a fool Malic."

My lap becomes wet with her sadness, with her pleading; each tear so warm; heated with emotions—tears so convoluted with anger and sadness, I fear they might burn holes in my confidence. Her sobbing frustrates me, making me yearn for a drink, making me excited for this next retreat.

I bet my boys don't have to deal with this from the girls they fuck; shit, this whole argument is the main reason Illegra is not officially my girl. This soaked lap is the last alarm, and that's it for me. I grab Illegra by her shoulders, lifting her out of my lap, forcing sapphire to onyx.

"What is it you want? Hmm?.."

Illegra looks into me with the sapphire of confusion, this helpless gander that only seems to infuriate me. I have never put my hand on any woman; this is the first time I am to grab a woman with such force, and I immediately loosen my grasp.

"What? What do you want? Some sort of social post or some pictures of us on a platform that makes money off our image? Are you crazy?"

An elixir of pure sadness streams down her alabaster skin, eyes swollen by a sadness I can't seem to understand. I try letting the words out as soft as possible, hoping to make up for such a peculiar outburst. Sapphire looks up to onyx, filled with so much bewildered pain. She can't understand why what she wants won't happen, and I can't seem to explain.

"You know I can't do that, Leggy." You know my whole career counts on networking and ...."

Illegra interrupts.

"It doesn't have to be on the internet, social media, or whatever; I just want to know that you fucking care! ...Just tell me. Just let me know that I am your girlfriend. I want to know you love me, damn it!"

As Illegra cries out in lugubrious desperation, begging me to say words that I can't seem to find. There is a quiet rage in her voice, but her distress takes precedence. My lap has become so damp with the melancholy of our relationship, only making me yearn for a drink that much more, making me irritated.

We sit still for a moment, with Illegra's sniffles providing the only sound in the apartment. I have listened to what she said; I see what it is doing to her, and here I sit thinking of what it all means. Surveying the apartment, ascertaining the situation, then I finished putting on my right shoe, ready to leave. Getting up, she won't move from between my lap, so I step over her. The puzzled look and the wet sapphire are her last attempts to raise some emotion out of me. I look at her and feel nothing; I say nothing.

Illegra looks so lost, so confused, but can she see the onyx of my perplexion? Does she understand that my youth will not process love the way she wants me to?

It is too soon for us to be fighting. Too early for our relationship to have the moniker of "boyfriend and girlfriend." We are at a period fair too early for such hurtful vituperations that fall from her lips. She is reaching too hard--trying to turn this into more than it needs to be. Illegra is complicating things, and I don't need this headache.

Walking into the bathroom, feeling her eyes follow me as she finally begins to stand, my only hope is to get out of here as fast as possible. The evidence of coupling is looking into a mirror decorated with bras and durags. As onyx connects to the reflection of onyx, I begin my self-negotiation, the soliloquy of saps. Finally, head nods and mumbled words convince me that the best action plan is to leave for the "Rum." I wash my face, grab my coat, grab the car keys then head for the front door. Once again, Illegra steps in front of me, impeding my path.

"Are you going to say something? Anything?"

She tries stopping me, pushing me in the chest, but I move her out of the way with a stare. The stare, although Illegra knows I would never put my hands on any woman, my gaze puts fear into her. She moves out of my way, then follows behind me, speaking in a full-out rage—no more tears, no sniffles, just vituperation after vituperation all rolled within her accent.

"Is that it Malic? Are you going to just leave?"

I walk towards the front door from the hallway; I can feel her following behind me, but then she stops; I feel that too.

"Go ahead, leave. Leave! But I might not be here when you decide to come back drunk and alone…."

I can feel her arms crossed and her death stare. I can feel all of her emotions, mostly anger, all thrown in my direction. Then, finally, I feel a change in her disposition, and right as I get to the door, she says her final words.

"You are a FUCKING COWARD!"

It's the coldest thing Illegra has ever said to me. It stings much more than any other time. I stop for a second, contemplating words but quickly, I realize better not. I don't want to escalate this argument any further. I reach for the front door; the nob feels cold in my hand as I turn it; perhaps the heat interacts with my cold, complacent feel.

Pausing for just a second, I remember when we first began happily and filled to the brim with lust. Lust is a much easier emotion to handle and takes less work than love. There is no headache in lust, no arguments, only the feel, only the heat of anticipation, not this aggravation--the disquietude of this apartment, of this moment. The slight tilt of my head is like my sigh of sadness, my final "oh well," then I walk out, closing the door without even a glance back. I know only guilty looks will be staring out at me through the living room window, so I walk to the car without looking back, not even once.

Assuredly, Illegra will be viewing me, getting angrier with every step I take. Her sorrow has turned to rage by now, and if I stay, more than just regretful words might transpire. It is terrible to leave her like this, but I am also a single man who desires no drama and dislikes it when scenes become so deleterious.

I find myself wanting to stop; part of me wants to look back, but why? Why stay and deal with more drama? Why put myself through a shitty Friday night argument when I can be at the bar with the boys? Why waste any more time on this puerile interaction?

Instead, I continue walking, never looking back. I move forward with no glance of what transpired--without a feel for the moment. Finally, I adjust my shoulders on my path to the car, hoping to shrug off this doltish feeling, hoping to shake off the stench of a fool's coupling. It is time to hit the bar, leave this foolish night behind, and let my youth take the wheel.

Chapter 2: The Rum

Man, I can't wait to get a cold beer and escape the foolishness of this moment. Quickly I open the driver's door hopping in like Steve Mcqueen from "Bullet." I want to get out of here as soon as possible; who knows what is going through Illegra's mind at this moment; she is Italian, after all. I better get out of here before her mob sidekicks in and she "wacks" me, or worse. I turn the key to the ignition, then begin backing out of the parking spot. I take a glance at the living room window. As soon as I look up, I see the curtain waving side to side, a sign of Illegra's final attempt, signifying that she has stopped looking at me. For a moment, I feel hurt at the possibility of our end; my onyx becomes damp, but then I snap out of it. Let me turn on this Kendrick Lamar, crank it out loud, and get out of here.

"I can't believe women sometimes!"

The words I shout help with getting my frustrations out. Talking to myself is often how I spend my drives after an argument, blowing steam, shouting vituperations I would never say directly to Illegra, gripping and punching the steering wheel, and driving at unwise speeds.

"Like what the fuck does she want from me?"

Vexation bleeds from my lips as the music blast, and I begin to drive faster. I just can't wait to get to the "Rum."

"Grr, rawah…Ugh…What the fuck?

The growl out releases tension I've been holding back. I crank the music even louder, then grip the steering wheel with both hands attempting to pull the damn thing off. Hopefully, this music will drown out this moment, quiet my thoughts of Illegra, and slow the beat of my heart. There is nothing worse than showing up to a bar with a head full of steam; nobody needs that shit. Plus, I'm sure "The Boys" will be out, not to mention the women, the cold beers, the great music, the ambiance…This thought calms my peddle; a night out with "The Boys" always makes me feel better after an argument and no better place than the "Rum."

The "Rum," as we call it, has great music, pool tables, libations, and beautiful women, precisely what is needed after a foolish spat with Illegra. Taking my mind off the thought, I turn the music up as far as it can go, letting Kendrick's lyrics control my vibe.

♫I don't give a fuck. I don't give a fuck. I don't—I don't—I don't give a fuck… I'm willing to die for dis shit—I done cried for dis shit—might take a life for dis shit…♫

Kendrick Lamar's music is perfect whenever I feel defeated, and this song always lifts my spirit. His words are terrific; the ideal person to "bump" at a time like this. Kendrick is just as intelligent as he is hood, with ferocious lyrics and effortless cadence.

Considering the "Rum" is so close, my playlist aptly named "Fuck it" seems like the perfect mix of songs for this short ride. I check the ashtray for a blunt roach or one of Leggy's white girl joints; yes, the bottom part of the spliff. I light it, then take a slow, deep hit.

Having one of the best bars in town so close to the apartment might be why I am always tempted to leave. Perhaps I'd stay home to get yelled at, let Illegra vent, fuck a little, and then it would all float away on the sweat of rekindlement. But, I swear, ever since the creation of that damn Facebook status, women worldwide freak out about the state of their relationship. How does a mouse click or a tap on the phone carry so much weight? I can't wrap my head around why status and pictures mean so much to my generation. I'm sure our mothers and fathers never worried about relationship status; it didn't matter who knew they were together. But, back in their day, they had more significant problems.

What if Malcolm X was more worried about his Facebook status instead of fighting for Civil Rights? What if Gloria Steinem was more concerned about her boyfriend's Instagram feed instead of changing the face of journalism? How dumb has this world become in the light of the social media age?

If I am providing good dick if I take her out often and buy her beautiful things, what does it matter our Facebook status? Will a few pictures on Instagram make me love her any more or less? I don't understand what she wants from me.

"Why does she want to be up under me all of the damn time? Ugh, women are never fucking happy!"

I yell out, smacking the steering wheel as I drive; it feels like the perfect release of vexation. But, although my frustration feels good coming out, inside, the lingering question of "why" still festers. Why does it have to be so complicated?

Women are the loves of my existence, the muse of most creation, but I will never "get" women for the life of me. It seems that sweet guys get a raw deal because women don't want them, won't give them the time of day, but then less interested men get linked up with the clingy types; it never seems to line up. A woman can never just let you chill and hang with the boys; they want to be up under you. If you choose to watch a game, they want to be in your lap. If you don't text regularly, you are accused of cheating or being a "fuck boy." Women push their insecurities onto men, which eventually pushes us further away.

I bet if Leggy wasn't hassling me about our status, I'd be home right now. I'd be with her, ready for lovemaking, movies, ice cream, and in no particular order. Instead, here I am, driving to a bar, hoping to escape the drivel.

Maybe the single life is a better route? Perhaps the only road is the single road? Freedom to hang with the boys, play ball, hit bars with no worries, no pissed-off women, and no long arguments. Of course, we all seek companionship, but is it really worth it?

Driving up to the "Rum" parking lot is a quick fix for my wavering mood. Now, most folks would be discouraged by a full lot and big crowd, but my view is the onyx of potential. Seeing all of the cars and people, my frustration begins melting away. Every night is a good night at the "Rum," but Friday night, nothing beats a Friday night.

It's like "Cheers" in the eighties, a nice bar full of hot young people and libations that just keep flowing. People from all walks of life come to the "Rum," and Friday nights bring out the most colorful characters.

People come to blow off the steam of a long work week, the freaks pop in to find their new "daddies," and for the boys I know, we come to steal the freaks before the "daddies" can ever get a taste. It is our stomping ground, our local watering hole; for the "boys," there is no better place to take our frustrations out, and the "Rum" is the perfect spot to take my mind off my most recent female altercation. I can't wait.

Yeah, some ice-cold beers with the "boys" are all I need at this particular moment; speaking of my boys, let me grab my phone and see where these two fuckers are. Dee, Alex, and I rarely miss a night out together, and when the boys call for a meetup, it's all hands on deck. I need the "boys" right now; girls need their girls, and well, the boys need their boys. The times the "boys" and I share often trump any negative feels. We're clowns, and once we get around each other, watch out. We are like a walking locker room; vulgar, immature, full of yo' mamma jokes, and brotherly banter; I could use some good "clownin" right about. now.

Latin words make the bar's actual name, but the "Rum" is what we call it; it's what everyone calls it. I don't care if you live on the Upper Westside or in the Lower Valley; everyone who is everyone knows about Friday nights at the "Rum." You are either here or wish you were here. This place is always packed and full of people, and driving around this parking lot will put most in a flummox, but my excitement helps calm that irritation. A few spaces seem vacant over in the back, so I drive past all of the folks walking, yelling, and conversing about their expectations of the night. As I view their enthusiasm, it fuels me, excited to see my favorite bartender, and excited for this otherwise vexing night. Finally, I find a spot, park, then look for my phone.

"Where the fuck is my phone?"

An outburst of frustration is uncommon for me, but tonight, Illegra has a brotha feeling all iffy. I continue searching the car, becoming heated by the mess; I am shouting out in irritation, cursing, all-around having a mini-tantrum in the middle of this parking lot. Digging around this miniCopper, searching for my phone proves to be the stuff nightmares are made of. The clutter created by two twenty-something grown babies would drive any parent crazy. Illegra's make-up, my basketball shorts, candy wrappers, change, comic books, a tie, a bra, but no phone. Kendrick still bumps on the stereo, both car doors are open, and I am frantically searching all areas, throwing debris, causing a scene, then I hop back in the driver's seat out of breath, fumed by frustration.

Onlookers view my frantic search as they walk by; an amalgamation of beautiful eyes looks at me, feeling my pain, understanding how it feels to be without a phone. In this black and red miniCopper, there are only so many places my phone can be, so I search, and I search, but still no phone.

"Damn it!"

I'm pacing back and forth, waving my hands in the air, howling at the moon. I search the car one more time, check my pockets like a mad man, but no luck.

"Fuck!"

The outburst gets looks once again, but I don't care. Finally, after one more search, I come to terms with the fact that my phone must be back at the apartment. Stupid. I must have left it on the desk or something, maybe in the bathroom, possibly by my chair, regardless my phone is not here. I forgot my phone; I fucking forgot my phone, and it is probably in the hands of Illegra right now.

Is Illegra smart enough to break into my phone? Probably. Should I be worried about what she might find? Most definitely.

"FUUUCK!"

I scream one last time, letting the whole world feel the full power of my chagrin. I'm not going back to the apartment to get it, so that thought quickly skates by. Not having a phone is like losing part of your brain in today's world, but there is no way I am going back to the war zone I just left. So I sit in the car, steaming, close my eyes and listen to Kendrick.

It's hard to tell if I am more pissed off about forgetting my phone or that I might have left a relationship time bomb back home. Kendrick continues to play, then I lift my head from the driver's seat and check myself out in the rearview mirror. My most recent purchase is a pink bomber jacket; I can see the pink shoulders in my reflection. The sight of the pink bomber inspires a closer look, so I flip down the driver's side visor; time to prepare myself for my grand entrance into the "Rum."

The pink bomber jacket has an Oriental floral decal covering the entire back; it's fresh as fuck. This enchanting hand-stitched portrait of a Pelican surrounded by cherry blossom trees is very detailed and unlike anything anyone has ever seen. Such a fresh bomber jacket, I can't wait for the eyes in the "Rum" to get a load of me. If I can't have my phone, at least my fresh look will take my mind off of this silly fuckin night. Grabbing my Burberry cologne from the center console prepares me for any future female interaction. First, I spray some on my neck, then sprinkle some on the fingertips of my index and middle finger. Next, I rub the two pairs of fingertips together, then pat the cologne on the back of each earlobe. It is a trick I learned in college; it always gets a woman's attention. Women go crazy for a brotha that can dress well and smells good, but one must also have an edge. Most men spray the cologne on clothes, but this is all wrong; a much better aroma comes when the cologne hits the skin. After all, scents last longer on the body, and the smell behind the ears gives women a pleasant aromatic surprise when going in for the hug. But, hey, I am a single man, and have to keep a few tricks up my sleeve.

I pop in a few Altoids and look at my face and hair; I'm feeling good. Fresh breath, fresh clothes, fresh cologne; they say, "Never judge a book by its cover," but women never really go for that ole' wise tale, so I always make sure the cover catches them before they can ever read a page. Turning off the car, I look at myself before turning off the lights, then head out. It is a Friday night, so, "Beep—Beep…Beep—Beep." I double-check when hitting the car alarm. Illegra already wants to kill me, but if anything happens to this car, "Forget about it." With all of these people boozing and doing what they have to do to get what they are out here trying to get, I don't trust it. I take one last look at the car; it feels like a last look at Illegra, then heads towards the entrance.

Walking up to the doors, it is easy to see what kind of night this is, and as I walk through the Victorian pillars of the entrance, the crowd's electricity grabs me. The "Rum" always has this high-classed "Cheers" feel; this nostalgia is felt whenever one has a neighborhood hangout. I know I am a little young to reference Cheers, but I know what a neighborhood bar feels like, and for me, this is that bar. Hell, I'm the Norm; I have my own seat, the bartenders always have a beer waiting for me, and the few times Illegra has kicked me out, this is the first place I head; it's also the first place she looks. But don't be fooled by my "neighborhood" hangout; it is much more than that. The decor alone has much more class than most bars and clubs; the "Rum" is upscale and decadent—an authentic palace created for debaucherous nights.

Apparently, the owner is from Europe, so he takes the bar business to a new level. It's like a librarian's wet dream in here. Wooden bookshelves wrap circularly around two floors, not one wall without books. As you walk in, on the bottom floor are four fantastic mahogany pool tables off to the left, elevated from the bar area. These pool tables are always packed, and the waitlist is at least an hour or two long; it's like Billiards and Babes over there; people playing and people watching. Much like the Colosseum, this three-hundred and sixty-degree layout makes the "Rum" very appealing to the eye. Around the massive oval bar's perimeter is dome-like seating and cocktail tables, each row higher than before, all facing the bar. Everything from the bar to the bar stools, even the perimeter banister's railings, all mahogany, making for a place that holds a lot of prestige. The beautiful maroon wood always seems freshly finished; wood grain so dark it perfectly accentuates the obsidian metal that serves as the perfect gating and metal fixtures. It's very Victorian, dated; the entire place has this ancient royal feel. Never before the "Rum" have I seen mahogany paired with obsidian metal so beautifully, a majestic pairing; Anne Rice would swoon.

Upstairs, more bookshelves that are even bigger than the shelves on the ground floor. Each book is leather-bound, each bookshelf mahogany; the entire place smells of leather and rich mahogany. I imagine ancient libraries smelled of this, the aroma of this excellence, the aroma of divine dignitaries. There are rows and rows of tufted leather sofas facing each other with mahogany coffee tables for dining and drinking placed between them. I glance upstairs, then look over toward my favorite bartender.

Getting to the bar from the entrance, you walk forward about ten feet, then down eight rows of stairs. The massive oval bar area serves as the main attraction for the entire place; I always feel like a gladiator walking into a match. The liquor shelf is enormous, a fantastic centerpiece splitting the oval bar in two, standing what seems like a hundred feet high. This massive shelf has just about every liquor you could name and even more that you couldn't. Alcohols from all over the world, beautiful bottles lit up and reflecting the crystal chandelier. The only parts of the bar that are not in the circular Colosseum-like style are the billiards area to the left of the entrance, the rectangular seating area upstairs and downstairs, and the area catty-corner from the entrance where the kitchen and the bathrooms are. The "Rum" is truly breathtaking; not your typical hangout, the ideal getaway from angry girlfriends.

I can smell it in the air, the night, the anticipation, the feels needed to forget about that silly fight. The music is bumpin, my heart is bumpin, this is my vibe. Being here almost makes me forget the colossal fight Illegra, and I had. I glance at the bar to see that my seat is open, then begin my strut down to the main event. Viewing all of the eyes is my favorite part: the colors, the gleam, the way they look into me as I look into them. I walk around slowly, letting everyone see that I am here, giving them a nice look at my fresh fit. Braxton spots me, emerald connects to onyx, and that's my cue to head to my seat.

It is always a magnificent sight to see the "Rum" on a Friday night, but the women in here tonight only add to the beautiful decor. Looking around the bar, this is precisely why I rarely bring Leggy with me; hell, all guys leave their girls at home. This city really has the gambit of beauties, and they are all out tonight, tall, short, curvy, black, white, vanilla, you name it. Even the bartenders are breathtaking women, all except Braxton, of course. And the cocktail servers, forget about it. On most nights, the cocktail servers are the most beautiful women in the whole place, maybe the entire city and tonight is no different. I have my seat right by the server's area for that particular reason; the view is impeccable.

Taking the long way to my seat, walking around the bar, looking at all of the faces, all of the talent; I feel glad to be out. As I look around, I almost forget the fight between me and "Leggy."

"Leggy."

"Leggy" is the nickname that Illegra has had since childhood. She is pretty tall, and kids can be cruel, I suppose. She doesn't like the name, so I typically save it for when I'm picking on her or trying to be cute. But enough of all that, it's time for a cold beer. Time to forget about the nonsense, the harsh words, time to forget the shitty feeling in my stomach and try enjoying this night.

With so many people around the bar, I'm surprised that Braxton could save my seat. I walk past three women who look like Charlie's Angels or something; I give them a look, a nod but nothing more. Got to play it cool and not show too much interest; have to be chill and not show my frustrations; women have never much liked that sort of thing. It shows weakness and uncertainty, and women, at least the woman that I go for, do not like any sign of weakness; it's like they can smell it on you. One must be as cold as a shark when attracting women on a Friday night. One must stand out and look sharp, but most of all, one must be a mystery. Nobody in this town wants it too easy, and those men making the first move too soon often look "thirsty." So I continue to my seat, looking, winking, but nothing more.

"Hey, Star."

I blow a kiss to one of the cocktail waitresses as she walks drinks to a table.

"How's it going, handsome?... Great to see you again."

The smile on her face makes my heart flutter. Star is a stunner and one of the waitresses I flirt with the most. All of the servers love seeing me on nights like tonight; I'm much better than most regulars, I tip well, I'm funny, and let's face it, I'm not that bad looking either. I made it a point to befriend all of the waitresses and most bartenders, so everyone loves seeing me. Tip 1: Always make friends with the staff; it makes getting drinks easier that way; that's my motto.

As I approach my seat, which is still empty, I'm stopped by this fucking guy Chris. Chris always seems to find me in a crowd, no matter where we are. I swear I could be in a group of millions, and this flash fucker would still spot me.

"Yo kid, what's good? Wasn't expecting to see you here tonight…"

Chris says, kind of smug, but I'm not sure what he is getting at. I don't hate this guy, but I don't like this mutha fucka either. It feels like when Doc Holiday met Johnny Ringo. Chris continues.

"If I were you, I would be at home with "Leggy," on some "Netflix and chill" type of situation. With a lot less Netflix and a lot more chillin, if you know what I mean."

His smile irritates me, but the playful elbow jab to my ribs almost sparks a flame. Chris has this shit-eating grin on his face like he made some superlative or great jape like we are friends or some shit. But, in all actuality, he is the Hector to my Achilles, the Iceman to my Maverick, this mother fucker is the Batman to my Joker; I could give two shits about this guy.

"What business is it of yours where my girl is? You had your chance, and you blew it, let's just leave it at that."

I turn to walk away; the last thing I need is this silly fucker getting under my skin.

"Is she even your girl?"

Chris grabs me by the left arm as his words sting more than his grip. I yank my arm from his grasp; his hazel sparks fire in my onyx--these flames of protection. The room begins to spin as I look deep into the hazelnut iris of my nemesis. Deep within that hazel hue, hatred is developing, a hatred that seems more diabolical than ever before. Chris looks into me as though he wishes to harm me, as though his anger is brewing.

"You better be careful; a good woman like "Leggy" won't wait forever; trust me on that."

Chris's warning was not sincere but snarky--a snarky remark that hits me in the gut, then I walk away with my pride dwindling as what he says might very well be true.

But forget that idiot, Chris; I can't believe my eyes when I look to my stool: Some old guy now takes the chair that was empty only moments ago. Immediately I look back at Chris, viewing him as he walks, mad at what our interaction has cost me. Just another reason to hate that fucker. I look to my seat. I see the old man; what will I say to this old fucker?

I look over at the old man nervously, unsure of what to do. The old man has to be sixty or seventy or even eighty years old; it can be hard to tell with

Ebony folks. I always say, Ebony, don't crack unless you do crack. Shit, about the only times you can figure out the age of an Ebony person, is when they are really young or ancient; either way, this old man is in my seat.

I love that seat. This seat the old man sits in is perfect for multiple reasons. First, it's the seat closest to the cocktail waitresses; they come to pick up their orders, I get to flirt with them, eavesdrop a little; the bathroom is just behind me, closest to the seating area, easy to get to, and not to mention on busy nights like tonight, it can be tricky getting a bartender's attention, so my seat alleviates that difficulty. This seat puts me right in the action, girls, drinks, easy access; bartenders always give me focus in this seat. Finally, I see a sea of women gathering around this side of the bar. There are always women hanging around Braxton; women come to possibly get free drinks or flirt, or both; there is always some lovely scenery on this side of the bar.

The look I give Braxton asks, "what's up with this?" as I look at the old man, but Braxton shrugs me off, places a Heineken in front of me, then goes back to work. One of the waitresses I know looks at me, then giggles before walking off. Her giggle pokes fun at my current predicament; I give her an irksome look. Oblivious to the whole situation, the old man continues sipping his cocktail. From the looks of it, it is some sort of whiskey or scotch drink; it sits on a saucer plate, and without a care in the world, the old man sits on my stool.

How pompous does this old man have to be to not have his cocktail on a napkin or coaster but on a damn plate? Give me a fuckin break. I have never seen this old man before, nor have I seen a cocktail with its own seat.

The old man sits hunched over as most older men do, but he has broad shoulders. From his stature, I can assume that he must have been athletic at a younger age, more than likely basketball or football. He wears an all-black Kangol flat cap, brim to the front, which appears to unleash a white-haired chin strap that connects to a perfectly groomed goat-tee. The old man seems tall, at least 6'2", 6'3", and as I said before, you could feel a hint of dated athleticism. He's dressed dull but sharp; has the look of money. The black sports coat with purple stitching draped on the back of my barstool reaks of minimalist chic that is quite expensive in this city. The old man's shirt is a black polo-style but seems to be of better quality than anything Ralph Lauren could ever produce. His black pants seemed sharp but straightforward, and although I couldn't see what shoes he was wearing, a stench of money was all over this old man.

The old man looks well put together for his age, and then I look closer. His watch blinds with such glare that it literally steals time. I find myself completely mesmerized by this beautiful watch, by the color of it, by the movements, but who is the old man?

Chapter 3: My Chair, His watch

The old man has neither a grimace nor a smile; he sits on a barstool; his drink sits on a saucer dish. The old man has no care for what happens around him and no intention of making small talk. Although the "Rum" has yet to hit capacity, it is crowded here. People drink and talk all around the old man; waitresses collect drinks on his right, a fumbling patron kicks his chair on the left; still, the old man never reacts, utterly unfazed by the world that revolves around him, the old man sips his brownish-pink cocktail unaffected. The ensuing chaos of a Friday night rush seems inevitable, and still, the old man is unshaken. He sits with his drink, takes a sip, then places it on the saucer.

Who is this old man? Why is he here?

In all fairness, he doesn't have the look of a frail old gentleman counting the days until his bitter end. No, this old man has a sort of 'Ebony Everlast' feel. He looks around sixty or seventy, which undoubtedly means he is much older. His lean on the bar is not just for style; more than likely, he has an ailment, making his lean more comfortable, justified even. But still, he's too old for this crowd of ex-frat boys and outdated sorority girls, and I can't imagine he is meeting someone here. I look around the bar hoping to send the message that I am engaged in the night, hoping not to allude my intrigue to the old man.

I wonder how I could get the old man's attention without seeming too anxious? On any other night, I would walk away from the man in my seat; no need for confrontation. Most nights, I would find another spot at the bar or even get the bartender to remove the person on my stool, but he is old, and his watch has my attention. Curiosity stirs as I stare at the beauty wrapped around the old man's wrist; it has my attention just as time often does.

I like timepieces; I always have. I like watches and pocket watches, oversized clocks, clocks on the side of buildings; I enjoy sundials and ancient ways of recording time. I even love the little clocks shining, accentuating the leather interior within expensive cars. I have always liked old clocks and new watch technology, and I like time. Upon seeing the big clock featured in "Back to the Future," I was fascinated by Doc Brown and Marty's manipulation of time. I often thought about watches and clocks, contemplating the power of time. Oh, all of the fantastic places one could go to if one could control time. If one could control time, one could control life; I have always thought that.

The very reason watches and clocks have always been a hidden obsession is my complete adoration of the science that goes into a timepiece—these fascinating and intricate works of art, the micro-motors that control time; how beautiful they are. What incredible detail and skill it takes to create a watch—what intelligences one must have to build and maintain time, even the sound of a clock or watch can steal me—a sound that has never had to evolve—a sound that has withstood the literal test of time; but watches have evolved, and the world around the clock has developed, yet the tick-tock of time stays. Time is a perfection that has no equal, which is the true beauty of time—that is what makes time so fascinating.

But then, beyond my being a chronophile, I can think of no better way of completing an outfit. A person can be a hipster hobo, but if they were to wear a Bulgaria Magsonic or like a Mainers Du Temps, their appearance transforms. Likewise, any person can wear rags, but a Paul Newman Rolex Daytona will take them from hobo to king in a matter of seconds. I'd gladly welcome any of those magnificent works of timely art and thousands more that would make royalty swoon, but this watch the old man wears is entirely different.

I suppose if I wore a watch such as the old man's, the world could not bother me; the world would not move me. A timepiece such as his would never afford me time with ordinary people, and the monotonous meandering of words would only irritate me. If I were the old man, I would not want to hear anything from anyone, especially nothing coming out of the mouth of a gawking young Ebony man like myself. But still, here I stand; nevertheless, I wonder, how can I get this old man's attention?

The watch catches my eyes yet again like the seduction of an enchanting woman. Rose gold shines in the light stealing attention from an envious crystal chandelier; the face of the watch shows the complete inner workings and craftsmanship; it's like a living, breathing, royal pink city of lights. Spotting each movement makes me feel as though I'm peeking behind a curtain, getting away with something—as though I am witnessing time in its creation. With each second that goes by, every piece of rose gold moves; organized chaos; the chaos that only time can create. When one wheel rotates right, another goes left; if the minute hand moves a millimeter, the entire watch goes into a frenzy of collaborated action. Once the glistening of black leather attempts to blind my admiration, I begin to understand the old man's supercilious nature.

Never have I seen leather shine in such a way; the glow on the leather is as though each octagonal scale mark is its very own stage. This black, shiny, reptilian skin must be a rare breed specifically created to wrap around this man. I laugh to myself, tickled by imagination. I imagine they make animals specifically for this watch and for this man, a leather so decadent, so rich, specifically made worthy of holding time. This leather is the perfect dress for such a gorgeous timepiece; I look at the leather, the face, and look at the man; I must get a closer look.

Admiration has quickly replaced pubescent rage; after all, what is one barstool in a world of magnificent timepieces? As smitten as a sugar baby—as thirsty as all of the women here; my eyes stay glued to the old man's watch, and I need to know more. I can't help myself as I stare at the timepiece, adoring how each movement of the hands creates a symphony of action, which hypnotizes with each tick-tock of time. The watch becomes more intriguing than anything surrounding me; I am mesmerized and delighted by the sight of the old man's timepiece, and I have always been so fond of extraordinary watches.

"It shows tremendous responsibility and integrity. A great watch represents the type of man you might be."

An older man's voice echoes in my head as I stare into the watch. I've never had a father or even a father figure, but I am sure that this is what would be said. I'm sure that my father would have a whole manner of teachings as we would shop for a watch. As I look at the old man's timepiece, I can only imagine where the old man would take his son shopping for a watch, and as the pink ratchet wheel turns, I find myself in remembrance; in remembrance of a time when a father would have a son, and that father would take that son out to buy a watch.

I imagine it would be a warm day out in some city I could never pronounce. A town where we would be out of place but comfortable—welcomed even; a place new but inviting. We'd be accepted by all who walk by, and people would admire the relationship between father and son. My father and I would be new to the area, but never would we be novice. My father would walk me into an expensive watch store, have me pick from a thousand timepieces, and the sound of a thousand ticks would enthrall my mind. I would be in love with every piece of time, and it would be so hard to choose; I would look, and I would look, then after much debate, we would pick a matching pair.

Yeah, we would pick a matching pair, and we would drink beers, sip the finest scotch, and we would go to places we couldn't pronounce. We would spend time together, and we would love each other; my father and I would do all of these things together because that is what fathers and sons do, and someday, I, too, would do this with my son; I would do this with my son, and I would love my son because that is what fathers do.

Hypnotized by the watch's movements took me into a mirage, an untrue moment of remembrance, something so powerful and so potent, something more compelling than imagination. A father. A son. It is a story that was never written and never will be, but I could be a father, and I could have a son, and someday I could do that for my son. I could be the type of father who spends time with his son—the kind of father who buys clocks, watches, and timepieces—the sort of father who cares and who is there—a father who cherishes time because I would know the value of time; I would own clocks, watches, and timepieces, and I would know what time means. I would be there, and I would want to be there because I would know what it means to be there. After all, what makes a man a father is a man who is there. And I want to be that type of father; I must be.

At this profound moment, I realize that I must talk to the old man; I must obtain the secret to controlling time with such eloquence, and I must learn how the old man procured the watch and how I, too, could acquire such a marvel. So I snap out of the haze, mentally shaking off all the daze and craze that I have felt, staring into the face of time. I'm going to approach the old man, and I must, but how?

What can I say to this old man who does not seem to care in the world? I sit for a second, hoping to create the perfect ice breaker. I look at the old man's clothes, his Kangol hat, and his blazer on the chair; I search each inch of his clothing for the perfect opener. Then, finally, I look down at his chair. Oh, the stool; the stool is my in.

"Umm... Eh...hmm, excuse me. Sir."

A muffle of sounds and nervous words bumble out of my mouth. I feel like a kid hoping for an autograph from Michael Jordan or meeting Richard Branson or something; my nerves rattle. The old man takes the tiniest sip of his drink, barely lifting the glass to his lips, then places the crystal rocks glass back on the saucer. The old man smacks his lips as if that drop of liquor has quenched every bit of his entire thirst.

"Aah..."

The old man ignores me, letting the sound of his refreshment float off into the night. I feel ghostly as he savors the drink, unresponsive to my presence. Maybe he's deaf or something, can't hear me; perhaps the bar's music and chatter are too much for his old ears. Finally, as I am about to tap the old man on the left shoulder to grab his attention, he turns his head to look at me.

"Excuse me, can I help you?"

Irritation rubs the old man's throat.

"I just wanted to let you know that you're sitting in my seat."

I give the old man a slight smirk as his eyes fill with the onyx of observation. He looks me up and down with no reaction at all. The old man begins surveying the bar, looking for something, checking all areas, then turns his swivel stool back around to his drink

"Is that right?"

The old man speaks with no sense of giving a fuck; not even looking at me. Instead, he grabs his drink and then takes another tiny sip. This next sip seems to be even more satisfying than the last; a louder smack of the lips and even more refreshing, "Aah," a sound that shows a complete disregard for the person I might be. I tap my index finger on his left shoulder twice, then start again.

"I'm serious. This is my seat."

I add more bass to my voice, hoping to catch the old man's intrigue. I figure this would be a great way to break the ice with a wealthy man, establish a sense of power, let him know I am local, and show some sense of ownership before my barrage of questions about his watch. "Wealthy men respect authoritative people," I read that in a book once. The old man swivels his stool until he faces me; the fold of years past surrounds the deep onyx that connects to my onyx.

"Do you own this bar?"

His question shoves me back.

"No, I..."

"Did you build or create this fucking chair?"

The old man's vulgarity is calm, soothing, not rushed, like a slap of silk.

"Well, no."

I answer with a slight fear scratching my throat.

"And is your name on this particular chair?"

He blinks twice, tilting his head unamused.

"I mean, well, no."

My words come out as limp as warm noodles; my retort is just as weak as my reproach, and the old man knows.

"Then leave me the fuck alone. Take that seat right there, over there, or any fucking where. Sit down and chill the fuck out before I put your dick in the dirt."

The old man's impetuous delivery strokes thick layers of disbelief on my face. I take a seat next to him, speechless, almost thoughtless. The old man's quick rejection and vulgar words run rampant in my mind causing a subtle discomfort. Slowly I sip my beer, shocked, trying to mind my business. The angst created by this supercilious old man adds bounce to my left leg. If we were back in the 'hood,' cats would get shot for that. But we are not in the 'hood,' and I am not exactly 'hood' myself.

My youth has me heated, but the watch has my intrigue. As I drink my beer, my eyes peer over to the old man's timepiece and the crystal rock's glass he rotates. The old man is getting to the end of his drink, only a thin layer of brownish pink liquid funneling at the bottom of the glass, so I ask, "What are you drinking?"

"Okay young buck, I'll ask again. Are you the owner?"

The old man asks without the search for an answer; his face has lost all patience. I quietly shake my head.

"No, I don't think so. You know how I know?"

My face is as blank as my mind, with no words for retort.

"Look at you; you think you have it going on, but you don't... Your hair is dreaded up like a fucking pineapple; you wear ripped jeans in hopes of being rugged—looking like a George Michaels's music video. This pink bomber jacket screams, "I need attention"—attention that you're obviously not getting."

The old man motions the absence of female companionship, completely mocking me.

"And those Jordan shoes don't even match what you wear. They are beat up and overworn, much like you. No wonder you are drinking a Heinekin at a craft cocktail bar."

The harmonious roar of this old man drops my confidence level to that of a cub, an imp, but still, he continues.

"The only thing you have going for you is this gray v-neck shirt that seems to fit properly and your goat-tee that must have finally grown in about a week ago."

The old man looks me up and down in disgust, then puts his hands up to the bartender, signaling for another drink. He takes one more loathsome gander at me, shakes his head, then turns to face the immaculate liquor shelf illuminated by the crystal chandelier. Defeated, I sit next to the old man and sit back. This old man has ripped me apart with words that almost cut deeper than Illegra's proclamation of me being a "coward." I take a large chug of my beer, contemplating my newest escape. But, man, I'm getting torn to shreds tonight; I just can't win. I sit still for a minute or two, looking into the liquor shelf with the linger of embarrassment creeping up my spine. Then, just as the old man was before I interrupted, I sit.

I sit unaffected by the world; the sounds of the bar bother me not, the chatter can't be heard, only the old man's words echo in my ear, putting me in my place. It's hard not to feel sorry for myself after that, and after this night, I suppose I should leave before interacting with this old man any further. He doesn't want to be bothered, and I am not sure I have any confidence left for a Friday night at the "Rum." My pride has fallen out on the floor, and I'm not sure I'm willing to retrieve it.

The final chug of Heinkien is long, meant to wash the sour taste of the old man's words down. The beer's bottom is warm, mainly saliva, a nasty way to end an already bitter night. I place the bottle on the bar, more disgusted with myself than the beer; I go to motion Braxton for my tab, contemplating this silly night, but then I feel the onyx of the old man beaming at the back of my head. I recall my forgotten phone searching through my empty pockets like a distant memory. Typically in moments like this, people pull out their phones to act busy and take attention off their loneliness, but I'm not afforded that privilege on this night.

"What's your deal, young buck?"

The old man's inquiry is ignored. I wonder if my disregard has the same sort of bitterness as the old man's did.

"Hey, owner. I'm talking to you."

He says with a bit of bass in his voice, and I can feel his chair turned in my direction. Nervously I look to my right and then say, "No deal, just out on a Friday night."

The old man nods his head in agreement. "Just out on a Friday night; yeah, I bet." He sips his drink then puts it back down on the saucer.

"And you are dolo?"

The old man asks.

"Dolo?"

My face wrinkled with confusion.

"Solo. By yourself. No friends….No girl… Who did you come with?"

He asks the question slowly, making sure I understand the nature of his words.

"Yeah, I came by myself, but I know a few people."

I adjust my seating, then point back in the direction of Chris and his group of friends.

"Yeah, right."

The old man laughs into his drink, echoing back out of the glass.

"You and that boy go together about as good as obesity and the Victoria's Secret fashion show."

He says side-eyed, out of his glass, then takes a sip; we chuckle. The old man puts his glass on the saucer as we turn back to face the bar.

"I witnessed your interaction with that boy before I took your seat."

His sarcasm pairs perfectly with an elder giggle.

"Is there some bad blood there?"

The old man asks, doing a better version of breaking the ice, slicing through the tension I've created.

"Yeah, he was with my girl back in high school. Apparently, he treated her like shit but has always wanted her back... He's kind of a dick."

I smirk at the old man.

"Yeah..." The old man nods, "in life, you're liable to come across many unsavory characters; hell, you might even become a dick one day."

The old man's light push of my right shoulder implies I was being a dick and his side-eye suggests that he was no better.

The old man and I sit silently for a split; I look down at my empty beer, and the old man turns back to his drink. Should I order another beer, or should I go back home to Illegra? The debating mind of a man out of place and possibly out of time.

I sit thinking of what should be done, weighing the few options I have left. I order another beer, thinking of what the old man has said. This cold beer calms prior bitterness, and I'm always a little bitter when thinking of that fucker, Chris. I refrain from looking at the old man, clutching my new beer with both hands, thinking. Chris, my mind traces off for a second.

What a dick Chris is; I suppose the old man is right about coming across many unsavory characters in life, and Chris is about as tasteless as you get. Sipping my beer, the cold bite of hops coats every part of my throat on the way down; it is impressive how a refreshing drink can clear the mind. I look over to the right, noticing the old man's head bouncing to the music; he seems to have loosened up a bit.

Finally, realizing that the old man was just trying to engage with me hits the mind. I might have a chance to speak with him, and there will be no better opportunity than now to ask about the watch. I lift my beer, drink down some confidence, then turn to the old man.

"So old buck, what's that around your wrist?"

The words feel brave sliding off of my lips and into his ear. The old man looks down at the watch, and then I.

"O, this right here, this is a watch."

He chuckles to himself after the words rumble slowly out.

"You young bucks don't know anything nowadays, do you."

I interrupt his grandad joke with an equally witty remark.

"I'd say that's not a watch; that's someone's house sitting on your wrist."

I give the old man a look, letting him know I know more than he thinks.

"You would be right about that, and a very nice house at that."

The old man begins admiring the watch looking at the night's reflection on the face. I lean in closer to the old man.

"Do you mind if I take a closer look?"

I offer my hand out for his approval.

"Sure."

He holds his left wrist up in my direction, and I lean closer.

As I hold his left wrist in my hand, the word beautiful never comes to mind; this watch far surpasses beauty. To call this timepiece beautiful would be a tawdry representation of unmatched majesty. Even calling this masterpiece a watch feels cheap, like the prostitution of words. Looking into the watch's face,

I see the Rose gold hands looking like spears of mythical metals; each wheel of the timepiece shines as if they are constantly spotlighted. I find myself even more mesmerized by this enchanting piece of craftsmanship.

"Where would someone acquire such a watch?"

A feeble attempt at eloquence slides through my lips like the weak accent of a movie star. "The presence of money makes fools of us all," I once heard.

The old man looks back down at the watch as though looking deep into it will award him the answer; I patiently await the arrival.

"Milan."

He lets out calmly as if just saying the name had brought back a particular memory.

"I purchased it at the finest watch store in Milan, Italy; Mercanti D'Oro SRL… It's like walking into Mount Olympus and purchasing Zeus's finest lightning bolt, and the women…"

The old man puts his hands to his lips, mimicking what I picture an Italian man would do—kissing them.

"The women are magnifico; I make it a point to go once a year for about a month."

The old man says proudly.

"Haha, even at my age, I still have a bit left for those Italian women."

Lifting his glass, he takes a bigger, more satisfying sip.

"Aah.."

The old man's eyes float to the ceiling for remembrance, taking him out of this bar, out of this night, and back to Milan.

"I bet I can tell you what watch that is."

I challenge the old man, bringing him back to reality.

"Is that so?"

He asks curiously.

"Well then, Mach weiter."

The old man says, and he signals for me to continue with his left hand.

"Well, at first glance, I thought it might be a Bulgaria Magsonic, but once you allowed a closer look, I was excited to see that it is actually an Audemars Piguet Royal Oak Grande Complication...."

My pronunciation is hideous, but the old man understands and is somewhat impressed, so I continue.

"The face is an 18-carat rose gold case with a unique hand-wound movement. The glass is double curved sapphire crystal, and the dial is lacquered black inner bezel with 18-carat rose gold hands. The bracelet is a hand-stitched "large square scale" black alligator strap with 18-carat rose gold folding clasp."

My denouement is proud and full of confidence; you would swear I was selling the damn watch. The old man playfully claps his hand, peering at me with the onyx of adoration.

"Bravo…Bravo, but as one man to another, you pronounce it pink gold, not rose."

The old man smirks at me before taking yet another sip.

"Aah."

"How much did it cost, if you don't mind me asking?… Probably an arm and a leg, I suppose."

The old man looks for the answer within the face of the watch, or I think that's what his gaze intends; he wiggles his wrist, then adjusts in his seat a little.

"Well, I paid £741,600, which in U.S. dollars would be roughly about 840,000." He looks at me as I gasp. "I would say a bit more than an arm and a leg."

The old man winks at me, then we both chuckle.

The old man's accent cannot be placed, not European; I can tell he is American, but from the way he speaks, he sounds distinguished, with the tone of a well-traveled man.

"And where is it from?"

The onyx of interest takes me; this unrelenting curiosity pleading for more information, hoping that the knowledge will bring me closer to the watch.

"Well, it was created by the Swiss, which is why I said "mach weiter," which means "go on" in Swiss German… But like most things, I'm sure it was made in China."

The old man ends slightly disappointed with the last part, then shakes the watch back into place before placing his left hand on the bar.

"I noticed you are wearing the watch on your left wrist, but isn't it supposed to be on the right?"

My last question raises his brow. The old man glances at me, then looks down at the watch one last time. The wrinkle of his brow proves my little inquiry has brought back some attention that the old man might not have paid otherwise, a detail that only so few would notice. As he looks at the watch, he has begun to appreciate it even more than before, perhaps even more than weeks before.

"I'm left-handed, so I had them custom-make this left-handed version…Great eye, young buck, great eye."

The old man ends up more impressed with me than before. We sit for a moment, looking around the bar, hoping not to seem anxious.

"That was a magnificent young buck. I have to say I'm quite impressed."

The old man nods his head in approval of where this conversation has gone. He turns his stool to where he is facing me, looks me up and down, then looks at my beer. Startled by his gander, I say nothing. His onyx searches me, but mine flees the gaze.

"Now, there is nothing I can do about the way you're dressed, but at the very least, I can give you some drinking culture."

The old man motions his utter disappointment by pointing out my drinking choice.

"What's wrong with my Heineken? It's a classy beer."

"Yeah, about as classy as a pornstar in a sundress…." He chuckles.

"You need a real drink, something that will change you. You need a drink that will give you culture, great taste, and maybe even something more. You need a Sazerac."

As the words fall from his mouth, I can feel an instant approval of himself, this sort of elevation that kings have. I look back into his onyx, excited but lost, and all I can ask is, "What's a Sazerac?"

Chapter 4: What's a Sazerac?

"What's a Sazerac?"

The old man repeats my question with his head in hand, shaking in disbelief. He slowly pulls his right hand down his face hoping to wipe away the utter disappointment at my naivety.

"Man, young buck, I wish I had more time to show you the ways of the world, but we simply do not have the means."

The old man shakes his head, then places his hand on my shoulder.

"It's ok—it's ok, my boy; most bartenders don't even know how to make a Sazerac, so don't feel too bad."

The old man pats me on the shoulder with his right hand before grabbing his glass off the saucer with his left. He then turns back to me and begins again.

"But before we embark on this liquid journey, let me give you a little history about the cocktail you're about to order."

The old man displays his drink right before my eyes. I can't say I expected the night to go this way, but this old man has my time and intrigue.

"Back in 1850, the Sazerac," The old man still holds his glass in the air, examining it. "…made with Sazerac French brandy and Peychaud's Bitters was immensely popular and became the first "branded" cocktail. The Sazerac, the first cocktail that is, was created by the one, the only Antoine Amédéé…" The old man puts his left hand up, pinching his figures together as if it helps with getting the accent just right. "Peychaud. Antoine Peychaud was a Creole apothecary from the French colony of Saint-Domingue; what we now call Hati."

Although I'm unsure why ordering a drink deserves a history lesson, I figure I have the old man talking, so intently I listen.

"Peychaud took his knowledge of medicine and drug-making to create the first-ever cocktail. It will be noted that he's also Responsible for the creation of Peychaud's bitters."

Then as a teacher would a student, the old man gives me a look that asks if I follow. Immediately I asked a few questions; I know teachers always loved that. I clear my throat to make sure I speak with clarity, more pronounced because the fumble of words is unbecoming.

"So first off, what is Peychaud's bitters, and second, is this really the first cocktail ever?"

The old man looks at me, flummoxed by my lack of culture; he doesn't look too enthused.

"The original version, made in 1850, was rumored to be the very first cocktail, yes, but since I'm not a Vampire, you and I will never know for sure." He laughs a little, and I smirk before reiterating my question.

"But what are Peychaud's bitters?"

The old man checks me, putting one finger up, telling me to stop.

"Tick-Tick" He clicks his tongue.

"I can't give you my entire wealth of knowledge in one-night young buck, and you will taste it soon enough."

The old man speaks as though my question interrupted his thought process, then he continues.

"But I digress; eventually, good ole Peychaud came across the magic elixir Absinthe about 20 years after the original cocktail; he switched the recipe from French brandy to rye whiskey and Cognac, then added in the Absinthe wash. Peychaud mixed the two liquors with Peychaud's bitters, Angostura bitters, poured that into the Absinthe washed glass, then ended with the express lemon as a garnish, giving us the Sazerac; which is still an amazing cocktail almost 150 years later."

The old man finishes by putting his glass up in the air yet again, taking another close look at the cocktail, then takes a sip, the same as he has done all night. He smacks his lips like the kids from the classic Welch's grape juice commercial, then ends with an expressive, "Aah… It's good every time." The old man looks at me with a haze of excited intoxication, almost like he's leading me to a new ride.

It is very entertaining to see this 60 or 70-year-old man get so excited about a cocktail, and he knows so much. Knowledge often impresses me; hell, even the mundane intellect tends to itch my intrigue. I can spend hours talking about a multitude of things; I love learning something new, hearing something new; it all has a place in my brain; it gets my wheels turning. Ending, the old man put the glass down on the saucer dish.

"You see, young buck, a good man, dare I say a gentleman, should always drink something that has a little history. It builds character, whether it is a scotch, a great whiskey, mezcal, wine, or even some classic gins. Moreover, it holds a certain prestige."

The old man's voice is so distinctive that it could have been a commercial. The old man's accent can not be placed, but I can feel his intelligence carefully sounded out with every word, every syllable, something so harmonizing in his diction. He speaks and holds himself like a wise Morgan Freeman but has the look of an elder Denzel. There's prestige to this man, and for a young black man like myself, it is great to be in the presence of an intelligent black man.

"Well, damn, I think I might be ready for my Saza… Sazareck." The old man chimed in to help me out. "Sazerac. S. A. Z. E. R. A. C," I repeat the word correctly, and the old man approves.

"Now, I don't know where the name came from, but I'd say I know enough about this damn drink to have a few. As you get older, you will find that you tend to store all kinds of random knowledge in your brain, and, well, you will lose some. It's the churn of time; something always drips out."

The old man laughs a little to himself as I give a smirk and a nod in agreement. The onyx surveys me, looking into onyx, then he puts his hand up in the air, motioning to the bartender, signaling for Braxton to make his way over to me.

"So, what are you waiting for? Order your damn drink. I'll pay for it." The old man motions to me, forcing me to order a drink. "Make sure to ask for Woodford Reserve Rye." He demands, then starts again. "Also, another quick lesson for you young buck, a real man orders his own drinks even if another man pays."

The old man sounds like my father would, and I'm sure from the outside looking in, he resembles a father—a father giving a son vital life lessons, and I am taking these lessons. The old man's advice is well received as I turn to get

Braxton's attention. Braxton is at the far left of the bar finishing up with a customer he's been flirting with since I arrived. He spots me with my hand up, then heads my way. At first, Braxton grabs a beer bottle, but I wave my left hand no, motioning him to come down to me. Braxton makes his way to me, surprised that I might either be switching up my drink or leaving; either would catch him off guard.

"What's going, lad; ya calling it a night ?" Braxton has that concerned bartender look, the sizing-up look of mild shock that all local bartenders have. A bartender is always shocked when it is time for you to go, "Sorry to see you go," and all, but that same bartender is also aghast if you stick around to get hammered. I have never understood that logic.

"No, nothing like that, though I might order a cocktail for a change." Braxton takes a playful step back, then step forward toward me. "Whoa, baby boy is going to step out, time ta play wif the big fellas, aye?"

Braxton laughs while he leans with his right elbow on the bar, looking towards the old man and the waitresses, playful, pointing his right thumb in my direction. Braxton then places his hands on the bar giving me his full attention in that classic bartender stance. He's ready, and I might have Braxton's full attention for the first time ever.

Braxton is very serious about bartending. Some treat bartending as a job, a preoccupation, a hobby, but not Braxton; oh no, for Brax, bartending is a career, a calling; it is what he was made to do. Braxton moved from Ireland specifically to bartend in this city, and if that weren't a good enough indication, his outfit on a nightly basis would take you back to the old days of a grand ole barkeep.

Braxton is dressed in that classic, old-school bartending style; black button-up vest, white button-up shirt, sleeves rolled up to his elbows, with the tie, suspenders, and the whole nine. He looks like a hipster with his lumberjack beard, full-on with a handlebar mustache, long red hair that is put back in a ponytail; Braxton has this rustic, hard-working, classic look. His rolled-up sleeves expose his colorful tattoos, tattoos that more than likely cover his entire body. Braxton looks and sounds like a badass leprechaun-hipster who is ready to bust out a golden pot of magical cocktails and elixirs with his red hair and business dress. Emerald finds onyx, awaiting my order.

"So what can I do you for?" Braxton asks, intrigued, eager to work. I put my right hand to my chin, with my thumb and index finger in place, caressing my jaw back and forth. I look to the right at the old man, then back at Braxton. "I'm thinking I want a Sazerac." Emerald connects to onyx, sparking excitement.

"Oh—" Braxton starts, super excited. "look who finally decided to put on some big boy trousers—a!" Braxton claps his hands and whistles, causing a complete scene at the bar. His excitement makes me smile, and if I weren't so dark, my face would be flushed with embarrassment. I look over to the old man; he seems to be shying away from the excitement, leaving me to the order. He's allowing me to take credit for a drink he has suggested; no words, no interaction. The old man waves his left hand in a circular motion; he means I have forgotten something—urging me to continue with the order.

"Oh, and make it Woodford Reserve Rye," I confidently say. Braxton rolls his sleeve up even further to prepare himself. One more nod of approval from Braxton, then he turns to gather the supplies and crafts needed to make the cocktail of all cocktails.

The "Rum's" liquor shelf is a real sight to see, the stuff dreams are made of. It's filled almost to the ceiling with a world of liquor. The mahogany wood frame climbs so high it almost hits the beautiful crystal chandelier. The foliage intertwines, woven into each shelf as if witchcraft or myth or both had contorted each vine. Colorful lights illuminate each row and bottle, changing colors to the rhythm of the night. A feeling of momentous intimidation slaps me as I gaze up at it, but when Braxton grabs the rolling ladder, I feel unprepared.

The identical rolling ladders, as is everything in the "Rum," these mahogany ladders seemed to be blessed by Zeus. Like ladders from large libraries and fancy homes, they roll from side to side with ease, turning anyone into Belle momentarily. Frequently bartenders roll the ladders out to get bottles from the higher selves, "top shelf," as they call it and depending on the bottle, ring goes the bell. The ladders on either side allow access to the Platinum bell. The Platinum bell serves two purposes: It reflects the light from the crystal chandelier almost like a disco ball and obviously creates a ring. The bell ring lets the whole bar know that money is in the house, one thing that I definitely don't have. Seeing Braxton reach for the ladder leads me to believe this will not be a cheap drink, but the old man has this round, so no sweat. The Woodford is not too high up, but then Braxton climbs up even further. Braxton climbs all the way to the top, then rings the bell.

"My buddy Malic has finally gotten some balls and ordered his first cocktail!" Braxton yells out as he rings the bell, causing the entire building to react.

The bar crowd bust out into an uproar of claps, screams, whistles, and cheers. I feel bashful for a split second, but attention has never scared me too much. I take a bow and join in with a few claps before taking my seat. Braxton makes his way down the ladder with a bottle as green as his eyes. The emerald hue is beautiful, but when the light grazes the bottle, it makes a glare I swear could cut diamonds. It's not a blinding glare, more of an enticing gleam of seduction. The glow has this magnetism like this magical elixir was entrapping me, pulling me, wanting me. As he comes down with the bottle, I notice it has the shape of a skull. It is an intimidating bottle, especially for a person new to Absinthe, but there is still something inviting. I have heard of Absinthe before; I've seen actors drink this magical liquor in movies, and friends have talked about Absinthe, but never have I had a drink of it—nor have I even laid my eyes on it. Tonight is apparently the night, whether I am ready or not; Absinthe seems to be in my future. I look at the old man cautiously.

"What are you getting me to drink?"

Half-worried, half-joking, I look at the old man. The old man puts his right index finger to his lips, signaling me to be quiet.

"Shh…Just watch the process; it's almost the best part."

The old man instructs me, sounding as a father would when introducing his son to the wonders of life. Braxton's focus on gathering his tools, collecting the bottles, and lining up everything on the bar, is quite admirable. Like a mad scientist finding the right combination and putting together the suitable materials, Braxton organizes everything in his arsenal for this "magical elixir." All of this for one drink? He places the bottle of Woodford and a bottle of Cognac to his left, closest to the old man, then sets the green bottle to his right. Braxton leaves space between the bottles and then puts one figure up as if he has forgotten something. He walks around to the other side of the bar and then returns with a fountain in hand. "I almost forgot the "absinthe fountain," Braxton warns me before placing the fountain next to the Absinthe.

To the left, Braxton places a mixing glass, a tin measuring shot tool that has two ends: one short and the other long; both ends look like varying sized shot glasses. Next, Braxton places a long mixing spoon inside the mixing glass, and then he grabs two small bottles (Peychaud's and angostura bitters); afterward, he holds a crystal rock glass and places it on the bar. Next, Braxton pulls out what looks like a miniature wine glass next to the rocks glass. Then he sets a silver leaf-like utensil on top of the tiny wine glass and then looks over what he has gathered.

Looking down the row of all that Braxton has gathered puts the craft in a craft cocktail. It is complete alchemy; the excitement focuses on his face while he puts it together. At this moment, I begin to appreciate Braxton's love for bartending, understanding his love of the craft for just a moment. What awareness and slighted genius it takes to remember such intricate recipes. This is not ice in a glass with liquor poured over top; there's a dance to it, a rhythm that keeps him moving. This universal appeal pulls Braxton out of the world and into his own universe. This bubble of concentration brings Braxton to life;

bartending is Braxton's life. He rubs both hands together like he is about to perform perfect chemistry.

"Alright, you ready?"

Braxton asks as if he is preparing me for something unusual, something one of a kind, something life-changing. I excitedly nod my head.

"Come on, bruv, you can do better than that. Are you ready?"

Braxton's excitement grabs all surrounding attention; eyes from around the bar focus on the Irish mysticism that is about to be performed. You would imagine that Braxton is preparing to turn lead into a more luxurious metal by the way he commands attention.

"I'm ready." Nervous bass fills my air.

"Oh, that's not it. Come on, Malic, say it from ye chest. Let us feel the emotion, bruv." Braxton's rasp sounds so endearing; the love of his craft could be felt with every word.

"I'M FUCKING READY!"

Once again, the crowd around us goes crazy. Braxton claps his hands like a show performer grabbing all attention, and then he begins. Braxton first grabs a sugar cube out of a mason jar located under the bar of his well, then places that cube on top of the silver leaf. Next, he grabs the emerald skull, pulls the lid off, puts the cork top on the bar, and then smells the open bottle quickly. The scent alone seems enough to intoxicate him; then, he looks over at me. "Ever taken a whiff of tis Malic?" I shake my head no. Braxton hands me the bottle. I grab the skull's head's back and look deep into each emerald orbit, becoming even more enchanted by the liquid. It seems to shine brightly within the bar light, reflecting back the crystal chandelier. I put the open bottle to my nose and inhaled a deep, intoxicating whiff.

The music stops, all sounds around dissipate, and the "Rum" is at a standstill. No sound. No movement. Just me, the emerald skull, and Braxton, the bartender. I close my eyes, letting the aroma travel throughout my body.

First, it stings the nostrils, but not a poisonous sting like smelling something sour, but a pleasurable sting that clears all sinuses, forcing my eyes closed. Next, the aroma travels back behind my eyes; it means to tickle my senses, caressing my brain like no scent has ever done; the smell of exotic black lickerish coats my nostrils; it flows through me, beginning to coat my entire body with ecstasy. As the intoxicating aroma takes over, I feel one with everything—as though I were being taught something I should have always known.

"Smells good, right?"

Braxton grabs the bottle from my hand. He walks over to the miniature wine glass and then pours Absinthe over the sugar cube. As the liquid flows over the top, the sugar cube begins to shrink with each drop of Absinthe. Braxton pours it until the glass is a little less than half full. Next, he pulls the fountain placing the tiny faucet right over the top of the sugar cube's remains. The absinthe fountain comes filled with water and ice; the valve doesn't flow freely; instead, it slowly drips one drop at a time. Braxton leaves the fountain and then walks over to the mixing glass. I'm at such attention I can hear every drip of the fountain as Braxton begins the next steps. 'Drip.' Slow but steady. 'Drip.' The consistency of it. 'Drip.' It's hypnotizing. 'Drip.'

When at the mixing glass, he starts by pouring three dashes of the Peychauds into the mixing glass. 'Drip.' Peychaud's is a pinkish liquid that comes in a miniature bottle and pours out drop by drop, one at a time. Braxton now takes the hourglass-looking shot tin in hand after he pours in three bits of Angostura bitters, a darker brown liquid. Next, he pours the Woodford Rye with the longer end, filling it to the top, then pours the liquor into the mixing glass. 'Drip.' After that, Braxton flips the tin to the smaller end, takes the cognac bottle in hand, pours, and fills the short side to the top—he even spills a bit before pouring it into the mixing glass. 'Drip.'

Braxton now turns to the fountain, turning off the tiny faucet. He returns to the mixing glass and grabs the spoon out of it. Braxton takes a scoop of ice from his well, placing the ice within the mixing glass. He is not trying to fill the mixing glass and even pulls a few cubes out.

With the ice, the alcohol, and the bitters, Braxton begins stirring it all together. The way Braxton holds the long metal spoon in hand looks like a technique learned off in the mountains somewhere. I imagine Braxton acquired most of his talents from bartending monks off the coast of Tabet like his bartending is some ancient craft. Braxton's fantastic art had me mystified the entire time, but the next step catches my eye.

Braxton takes the leaf utensil off of the miniature wine glass. The sugar cube has disappeared, turning the liquid inside into the color of clouds. Still stirring the drink with his left hand, Braxton pours the Absinthe into the crystal rock glass with his right hand. Braxton's dexterity while mixing and pouring is like an act on Broadway or even in some circus. He stares at the crystal rock glass as he pours the clouded liquid whilst stirring the mixing glass. He then places the miniature wine glass down into the sink underneath the bar and wipes the area down with his bar towel while still stirring. Braxton continues mixing the glass a few more times before turning his attention to the rocks glass filled with Absinthe.

The rock glass liquid is a cloudy white color, not quite creamy, but not entirely clear. Braxton holds the crystal glass in the air observing it in the light. He then begins to swirl the glass in a circular motion. He contorts his wrist, swirling the liquor in the glass–he looks to be coating every part of it. Cloudy liquor slides from end to end, a thick liquid; it slides from the lip down to the bottom, much like cough syrup.

"What are you doing?"

I ask with curiosity, slapped to my face like kids and magic tricks.

"It's called an absinthe wash; I must coat the entire glass with absinthe."

To my shock, he coats the glass entirely and then pours out the remaining Absinthe into the sink afterward, leaving the coated glass on the bar. I am almost appalled that he just disregarded the Absinthe. Like nothing, Braxton dumps Absinthe down the sink, but in the rocks, glass remains just enough Absinthe to coat the inside of the glass, and a few drops create a very thin layer of clouded liquid. He then grabs a strainer while stirring the mixing glass a couple more times. He then places the filter over the top of the mixing glass and pours the contents into the Absinthe coated crystal rocks glass. Braxton looks to his right, then looks to his left.

"Trixie!" Braxton yells out to the other side of the bar.

Like magic, all of the noise and motion come back. Suddenly I was pulled

out of my trance and back into the bar. Commotion, music and people all come

back to life, and the clatter of glassware brings me right back to reality. I feel as

though I have opened my closed eyes. I look over to my right and see the old

man whose onyx beams in Braxton's direction.

"Trix, do you have my peeler?"

Braxton walks over to the end of the bar to retrieve his final tool. The old

man seems to be just as attentive as me; that or he really likes the look of Trixie.

Braxton walks back to me, peeling a lemon. He grabs a saucer plate, places a

cocktail napkin in its center, then puts the rocks glass on top of the napkin. Next,

Braxton sets the peel on a cutting board, then cuts the skin into a perfect

rectangle. Finally, he places the lemon peel on the saucer plate.

"Your Sazerac, my good sir," Braxton pronounces as he places his unique

cocktail right in front of me. I look down at the drink, almost scared to touch it.

Braxton quickly clears off the bar, then attends to an onslaught of customers. I

turn to the old man, putting my drink up for cheers, but the old man stops me.

"Don't forget to express your lemon peel." The old man demands.

"Ex-Express the lemon peel?" I ask, curious about what the old man means.

"That is just a fancy way of saying to squeeze the lemon peel into the glass; you get the lemon flavor inside the drink. Make sure to wipe the peel around the rim of the glass; your lips will be hit with lemon flavor, making the cocktail even more refreshing."

The old man's insight is well received, and he watches as I do as instructed. We sit face to face with our glasses in the air; then, we touch glasses.

"Cheers!" We say simultaneously as onyx connects to onyx.

As I put the glass to my lips, the aroma of all ingredients hit my nostrils. It's like an uncontrollable Mack truck of enchantment—the combination of everything rushing through my senses moves me. I tilt the glass back to take my first sip. Excitement parades my taste buds, and I begin to salivate. My tongue is surprised by a pleasant sting and tingle, and the roof of my mouth becomes coated, and as the Sazerac travels down my throat, each drop seems more satisfying than the last. This combination of taste and smell creates a feeling that can only be called theurgy.

Enchantment bites as the liquid travels; I feel each drop making its way to my stomach—every ounce. I close my eyes; my pleasuring senses are firing from all cylinders—my lips smack, my eyes open, and...

"Aah."

Chapter 5: Her eyes

The "Rum" is at full bump with almost double the people, volume raised,

lights flickering, and as I look around, this midnight might be the busiest I've ever seen this place. It's almost as if it has happened out of nowhere; sure, it was crowded when I first walked in, but right now, at this moment, this might be the busiest bar I have ever been to.

Bass hits each eardrum rhythmically—the bar has the vibration to it—customers get drinks, and crowds begin forming around the most famous bartenders. Women of all shapes and sizes swarm into the bar from god knows where. It seems this has all happened so fast, but I suppose the hypnosis of the Sazerac stole my attention.

"Thank you for the drink. I see why you like it so much."

The old man gives me a nod of appreciation, then we take another sip, "Aah."

"Can you taste superiority? Have you been able to get a good whiff of history?"

The old man looks to me as a father would a son; this endearing look, the look of a man feeling like a job well done. He is so happy to give a lesson—genuinely excited by this shared moment. How strange is this feeling that we share? How foreign but comfortable, like a city I could never pronounce.

"One thing I have to ask, did Braxton forget to put ice in my drink, or what?"

I present my glass in front of the old man's face. I am unsure if I missed something, or maybe out of excitement, Braxton forgot to put ice in my cocktail; regardless, only a lemon peel floated where the ice should be.

"Ha ha..No young buck, you wouldn't dare destroy a great cocktail such as this by watering it down with ice. Even a big, glorious ice sphere would destroy the aroma, the texture, and the taste of this drink. Ice would make this divine elixir some mortal drink."

The old man shakes his head at my uncultured inquisition. "Braxton made that Sazerac too perfection, young buck," he confesses, almost repulsed that I would ask such a question. I look to him retaining yet another lesson.

"Is it always busy like this on a Friday?" The old man's eyes survey the flow of patrons moving active like ants on sugar. "Well, I typically come here on Fridays, specifically for all of the talent, but normally I have my boys with me." I clear my throat. "But I do have to say this Friday seems to be a little crazier than most."

As if we have the same brain, the old man and I turn our stools to face the crowd. Simultaneously we turn to where our backs face the bar, getting a better view of the people inside. Over to the bar's left, we can see one of the pool tables packed with the typical Friday night douchebags and model types. To the back is comfortable seating—these tufted leather library chairs that look to belong to a monarch. This area serves as a place for the "cool kids," or people who think of themselves as of a more elevated caliber. So soon as that thought crosses my mind, I spot none other than that smug fucker Chris.

Chris is with his "cool" friends, making their best impressions of "important" people. They all take selfies on their phones and order trendy shots whilst sending judgmental looks to everyone who is not in their group. They remind me of a knock-off version of some Archie comic, dunces and ditzes, dumbing this intelligent space. Chris sends a hateful stare in my direction as he sips his drink; I sip my Sazerac as a sort of "fuck you" retort. The hate that this fucker has for me is real, almost palpable, but he could choke on ten dick for all I care—his stares won't ruin this Sazerac. "Aah.." But still, I view him through my Sazerac.

Chris has what I would call a "Carolton demeanor," he's the type of kid that has always come from money. He reeks of pomposity and holds his head so high up his own ass that his air is filled with pseudo supercilious thoughts. He is dressed like something out of a Lacoste brochure; bright polo shirts, white pants; he looks like a white boy switched bodies with a high-yellow sell-out.

Chris's caramel skin and hazel eyes only fuel our rivalry even more. It'd be easier to like the guy if he didn't look like a model and didn't have more money than god. Chris's father is one of those rewarded "uncle toms" that clawed his way to the top of a Fortune five hundred company, and now Chris gets to ride his father's coattail. I have tons of respect for his father, that man is a fucking legend on and off the basketball court, but Chris makes me sick. Everything about the person he is makes me feel disgusted, and the reality is this flash fucker happens to be the only real competition I have ever had.

"So, what is the story between you...." The old man pointed his glass at me. "..and that guy?" Then he points his drink toward Chris's direction.

"What do you mean?" I ask, trying to avoid the question, taking a begrudging sip.

"Well, he's surrounded by about five beautiful women, three other women that some might consider fuckable, and there are at least another 200 to 300 women in here, yet there he is, staring at you."

The old man wears the onyx of little judgemental intrigue, yet still, I avoid the question.

"You two remind me of an old western. The white hat staring at the black hat just before a shootout, tumbleweed doing its namesake justice."

The old man takes a sip of his drink, looking at me through his glass, possibly laughing on the inside. I, too, begin to laugh off the old man's honest depiction of my relationship with Chris, trying not to show frustration.

"Yeah, we are not fans of each other, Chris was my girl's high school sweetheart, so I suppose there is a little bad blood between us." I take another sip trying hard to avoid any further conversation on the matter.

"Your girl? Your none dressing, none drink ordering ass has a girlfriend?"

The old man says, giving me a playful smirk, a lite nudge of my shoulder, partnered with an old man wink. "Well, I am "seeing" his ex; it's not official," I say before turning around to face the bar, desperately not wanting to look in Chris's direction as I speak of Illegra.

I place my Sazerac back on the saucer, thinking of what I said. How foolish I must sound, claiming that Illegra is my girl when I won't even give her the respect of commitment. Why lie to a stranger by calling her "my girl"? I sit for a moment, thinking about what I really want. My brain stirs with more confusion than I had with Illegra back at the apartment. She is a great woman, she loves me, yet I feel there might be more than I deserve in life. What a bore my life would be if I tied myself down to just one woman.

I look into the liquor shelf hoping the answers can be pulled down like some magical elixir. Why won't I just make it official with Illegra? What am I waiting for? I take another sip, seeking, hoping the taste of answers will cool my budding disposition. Maybe it is as it is supposed to be, and eventually, the answers will materialize, and everything plays according to the grand plan. I shrug my shoulders and presume a fool's thought for a foolish boy.

"Aah..

"Answer me this; why are you just "seeing" this woman Illegra if she seems to be so desired by another?"

The old man asks as he turns his stool back around—I take another sip, still avoiding the question.

"Also, you better slow down on that Sazerac…."

The old man's look chills the Sazerac in my left hand with the bite of his warning cooling like frost.

"You see, the first Sazerac stirs the mind creating a daze of inquisition. The second Sazerac asks a particular question, digging deep within the psyche--pulling out the mind's raw materials. The third Sazerac answers the question you seek, giving the brain some much-needed clarity. And the fourth, well, not many make it to the fourth Sazerac." The old man's words instantly make me put the Sazerac back down on the saucer, concluding with a sinister laugh, almost haunting my night.

"Haha… That's what I thought you might do."

Something about this old man makes me listen; he has taken hold of my inhibition to show me something I might never have known, and I'm along for the ride. I look to him as a son would his father.

"So tell me why you are just "seeing"…" He puts his glass down on his saucer then puts both of his hands up to mimic quotation marks. "this girl?"

The old man is curious like a father would be about his son's love life. I turn my stool back around with my back to the bar, then wave my hands and arms out to the crowd, displaying all of the women. I look back at the old man and then say, "I'm weighing my options."

The words come out so proud that I almost believe what I've said. I look around at all of the beautiful women, wink at one lovely lady as she passes by, then I turn around to face the bar, continuing the conversation.

"Options, old buck, options. I am a 26-year-old ebony man living in one of the greatest cities in the world; I don't need to be tied down."

Feeling proud, I disregard the old man's warning about the Sazerac and take another sip.

"Weighing your option..." The old man dwells on the words for a second. "Aha, you are one of those "grass is greener" guys, aren't you?"

The old man's eyes look to be sizing me up once again—I can feel the judgment.

"I wouldn't say that, but if I've still got it, why not get it if you know what I mean."

Hopefully, the look I give the old man is as confident as my words.

"I've been weighing my options for almost 60 years now, don't weigh for too long. But, eventually, that wait becomes more than you can bear."

The old man takes a knowledgeable but foolish sip. There seems to be regret holding the glass to the old man's lips; this latent reaction of a doltish past. But surely a man of his stature could not hold too many regrets? There has to be some secret to getting to his level. Without a doubt, he is the wealthiest person in this bar; he probably owns multiple businesses and has definitely had his lay of the land. I'm sure that this man doesn't have to wonder about greener grass; he probably creates his own.

"But this Illegra must be a beautiful woman if your boy Chris over there still holds a flame for her—especially after all these years later."

This intense connection of onyx to onyx makes me wonder if he can see Illegra as her beauty flashes behind my eyes.

"Yea, she is a beautiful woman." The shine of her satin black hair glues my mind; her sapphire eyes, her alabaster skin, and for a moment, a whiff of her aroma climbs up each nostril. The truth is, I do love her, but sometimes it feels more important to be wanted and desired by others.

"Well, what does she look like, a young buck?"

The old man eagerly asks, almost noticing my visualization. Why is this old man so curious about my girl? I begin feeling weird about his most recent inquisition, but still, I oblige.

"She is tall, has long black hair and blue eyes—Italian, and has a New York accent...." The old man interrupts me by waving both hands up in exhaust.

"No, no young buck, I don't want you to just describe her as you would any other girl; those features could be thousands of women—hell, I have a few that fit such description tonight." The old man slaps me on the shoulder, hinting he has women. "The woman you described sounds ordinary, boring even; not the type of woman to create haters like...." He points his glass over in Chris's direction. "that fucker Chris. So order another drink, take a breath, and truly visualize this Illegra. You perform the visualization; I will buy the drink."

The old man's calm instructions ease me into my second Sazerac. I grab Braxton's attention and order my drink, with Braxton being just as eager as if it were the first. Once again, I find myself hypnotized as Braxton goes through the steps of concoction. First, pouring the Absinthe on the sugar—second, the water drip—third, the mixing glass—three dashes of Angostura—three bits Peychaud's—cognac—Rye—the stir—the absinthe wash—lastly, the rectangular lemon peel. Braxton places the drink in front of me, and now I'm ready once again.

The old man seems to wait, hankering for my visualization. Then, facing each other, we toast, take our sips, and, "Aah." We enjoy the sensations at almost the same time, in virtually the same way. The old man's eagerness almost has me spooked, but I figure what harm could it do—plus, he is buying my drinks.

"Ok young buck, close your eyes, and visualize." The old man insists.

At first, I close my eyes, and all I see is black; I hear movement, I feel the music, the bar's commotion breaks my concentration, and then it all stops. "Describe her to me.." I hear a voice that sounds almost identical to mine. The darkness of my mind clears as I begin to see Illegra. I see her as I've never seen her before.

"Her eyes are as deep as the ocean, yet as blue as the clear Hawaiian sky. It's almost as if all of heaven comes caught within her almond-shaped sapphires. There's a seductive innocence that reels you in at first glance. Her skin," I lightly shake my head. "her skin is an even balance of alabaster, almost porcelain. Oh, how it glows next to my dark skin, a skin tone that would make even Aphrodite green-eyed with envy. Illegra's iris' blue seems to be sharp as diamonds, perfectly complimenting her skin tone, which sends enchantment with every stare even when she is filled with anger—anger that I have more than likely caused. Her long, silky, satin black hair is so black it shines—shines almost as bright as her beautiful skin—almost like it would steal all the gleam from surrounding lights. Long hair, hair so long it reaches all of the ways down the crease of her perfect back equipped with back dimples." I pause for a second, picturing every inch of Illegra, reaching out to her, then continue.

"Speaking of dimples, the dimple on her left cheek and only on the left makes for the most perfect imperfection of an already mesmerizing appearance. The curvature of her face, from cheekbone to chin, is statuesque and dignified, much like her height. She stands no shorter than 5'9″, with legs that would make Adriana Lima emulous and unhinged. Illegra's skin is smooth as a cotton sheet in the summer wind, and with every divine word she speaks, you can feel peace crawl up your spine. She holds this refreshing aroma not captured in fragrance but a scent of all her own. She has a beauty mark," I can't hold back the smile as I picture her beauty mark, using my hands to illustrate her beauty. "right below her perfect lips, just above her chin, on the left side of her flawless face. Lips pink without lipstick—lips that, when puckered, make a perfect heart shape. Illegra has an hourglass figure of ideal proportion. Nothing exaggerated. Every part of her natural. From head to toe, a walking Goddess who walks with confidence and perfect posture. She is an east coast debutante of near-perfect design."

I open my onyx, the music, the movement all begin again, and I'm back sitting next to the old man. I take a deep breath, then look over at the old man. As though I have awoken from a dream, my onyx adjusts to the bar's lighting. I am not entirely lost, but this eerie and somewhat arousing sensation is coursing through my body.

"Now that is visualizing. That's not your typical run-of-the-meal description; that's more, so much more. That sounds like a woman you don't just "see" now, does it?"

The old man places his left hand on my right shoulder. Onyx connects to onyx as I feel everything the old man has said. I usually don't like all of this touching and profound talking, but this old man couldn't be more right.

Chapter 6: The Game

I can't help but feel that the old man might be correct in assessing Illegra and good women. Describing her, realizing what I have, begins to pound away at my mind--the jackhammer of dolts. I feel foolish; I feel so fuckin silly—I-I have to get the attention off of me. The old man and I have only just begun, yet he already has my brain forming in knots, and I am unsure if I am ready for all of these questions that develop.

What am I really doing? Why am I waiting so long to commit?

This personal inquisition is narcotizing; I feel lost in thought. Illegra is a great woman—she takes care of me, the love we make is out of this world, but why won't I make her my woman? Looking down at my Sazerac into the pinkish-brown liquid, I feel so fucking embarrassed that I don't want to hear myself think.

"So, what about you?"

I tip my glass toward the old man; he looks at me. His brow is furred, unsure of what I might be asking. "Looking at the watch, how you dress, speak, and drink, I'm sure you've had your fair share of beautiful women." I raise my glass and tilt my head, a gesture for the old man to spill the "beans."

"Where is your lady or ladies?"

I throw the final words in his direction, knowing that his chance to brag will give me some much-needed breathing space—helping me stay out of head. The old man takes off his black Kangol hat with his left hand, exposing his perfectly bald head. His head has a distinctive shine, almost reflective, with no trace of hair coming back anytime soon. The old man places the hat on the bar next to his Sazerac; I can't see the reaction on his face, but the slight raise of his white goatee is proof of a playful side smirk.

At this time, we're facing the bar letting the Sazerac fester; intoxication has yet to take hold, but I feel a stir. The old man looks into the pinkish-brown liquid, rubbing his left index finger around in circles, rimming the glass of his Sazerac.

Looking over at him, I notice a gloss of excited remembrance within the onyx of his eyes; a thick film of the past coats each eye as he grabs the Sazerac off the saucer. The old man takes another slow sip without saying a word; his eyes close as the Sazerac slides down his throat.

"Well, there have been a few in my day, young buck—there have been a few...."

The old man's happiness grows as memories climb into his mind, holding the Sazerac in both hands whilst recollecting a bit more.

"There have been many ladies along my path to this bar; some models, some singers, some rich actresses, married women, cocktail waitresses, and dare I say, I even rolled around with a princess or two."

The old man sits his Sazerac down on the saucer, then swivels his stool, facing me as excited as a high school jock. In my prior experience, I have learned that old men love talking about the good ole days and their conquest; they love reviewing the past and comparing exploits, always proclaiming, "We did it better." I assume we men like talking of such things because it reminds us of control when we were in control. But, unfortunately, so much of life is out of our control; things come, and things go. This is why past stories hold so much weight and staying power. Memories are stories that will always be yours and yours to hold.

"Back when I was younger, the "game" in me was dangerous, my boy, let me tell you." The old man chuckles as he adjusts his seat, using his right elbow on the side of the bar to gain some leverage as he scoots back into his stool. "Boy, I could sell a ketchup popsicle to a woman in white, ice to an Eskimo; I could talk a woman out of her panties way before I could buy them." The old man half-laughs.

"Oh, so you wanna tell me that you were some kind of Don Juan or something? A natural lady killer, I suppose?" I say before letting out a mocking laugh.

The old man nods with a smile hanging from his cheekbones. Even at his age, his cheekbones are so high and so round when he smiles; I imagine they play a part in making him look younger than he actually is, a defining feature. Sure he has an all-white goat-tee that looks like Santa groomed for the summer, and of course, the wrinkles and bushy eyebrows prove him being elderly, but this old man looks excellent for whatever age he is; 'Ebony Everlast,' remember.

"Shiiit, I probably have more game than you, even at this point in my life, young buck. Have you looked at yourself?"

The old man slaps my left knee playfully—laughing at my expense. His words begin stealing the grin from my lips, but quickly I recover with a spurious smile. Taking a look at what I wear compared to the old man's sharp dress; then take a sorrowful sip of my Sazerac.

Once again, this old man has choice words about how I am dressed, playful, or not. I look at the old man through my glass, losing confidence as the liquid coats my throat. Hopefully, this liquor will wash away the taste of my subtle contempt.

"Let's see...."

The old man says as he looks up towards the chandelier. He seems to look for a time when he was young, wild, and apparently getting any woman he wanted. I wonder what answers he will come up with, what exploits he has had, what he sees. Then the old man continues.

"The first time I visited Italy, now let me tell you, that was a trip, my boy." Onyx connects to onyx as the old man forms a smile brought to him by sweet memory. "I was out in Italy on a business trip. You see, I was trying to convince this rich Italian man that moving his tailoring company down to New York would be lucrative and could expand from Italy to the states with my help."

Pride scratches each side of the old man's throat as words float out into existence; I listen intently. Something about this old man makes me want to hear everything he says, and my eyes are glued in. Even though he has 'clowned' on me a couple of times, even with the loud music, the women, even the bar's commotion, nothing can steal my attention from this old man. It is an intrigue that I have only felt once before in my life, something so captivating.

"So I'm close to sealing the business deal; everything is going amazing until the Italian man that owns the company introduces me to his daughter Aurora."

The old man clicks his tongue on his teeth, sounding to the tone of "no, no, no."

"Outcomes this yellow-eyed, dark-haired, almond-skinned beauty. Aurora had this pixie hair cut that showed her beautiful neckline and bone structure." The old man sends the pop of onyx, emphasizing how gorgeous this woman must have been.

"She had a strut that would blow any man or woman for that matter away. It seemed as though she always walked in slow motion; every street was a runway, every light was her spotlight, and this stunning creature was the main attraction anywhere we went; I can see her now."

The old man shakes his head as if her beauty were a crime.

"Go on. Go on." I say, anxious to hear the rest of the story.

"As soon as she walked up, my business partner and best friend Devin gave me a look that said without words, "don't do it.""

The old man playfully grabs me by the shoulder, pulling me in, lightly rocking me back and forth.

"You should have seen Devin's face. It read, "please don't fucking do it," but it was too late. I already had the thought in my head that I must at least have dinner, or a drink, or coffee with this amazing woman. There would be nothing that Devin could say to sway me otherwise. Hell, I was even willing to go behind the Italian man's back to get a moment alone with his daughter. As I try to think of a brilliant way to ask Aurora out, her father beats me to the punch. The Italian man began explaining that his daughter was the last to be convinced before he would sign any deal."

Onyx stays locked to onyx as the old man continues.

"The next night, the Italian man invites Devin and me for some traditional Italian cuisine to finally sign off on the deal and make all reservations for our future business. Again, Aurora served as a mediator, and since I had the idea of merging our companies, the entire dinner was me talking to her directly, looking at her, conversing with more than just words."

The old man shakes his head again, letting loose a chuckle of disbelief.

"Damn, they pretty much set you two up," I say with a playful tone, assessing the circumstances of his past. The old man puts one finger in the air to say, "wait, there's more.

"The restaurant was Ristorante Vittorio, off of the coast of the Mediterranean Sea. Amazing seafood, the best Italian vino, and I could spot Tunisia in the distance from my seat, but those lemon-colored eyes really captured the night. Everything about that night was beautiful, but Aurora was heavenly. A more perfect setting could not have been set, and as I gazed at her, I saw my wants and needs."

The old man reaches back for his Sazerac, shaken by the memory.

"So, what happened?"

Eagerness flies out of my mouth so fast that I might seem desperate.

"What do you think happened? The Italian man left satisfied with the money he would make, and Aurora, well, Aurora, got to see me at my very best." The old man lifts his Sazerac to his lips. "Let's just say she was much more satisfied than her father; I can guarantee you that."

The old man pulls the glass from his lips, then tilts it toward me. We toast, share a smile, and then both take a sip.

"Aah.."

We sigh simultaneously.

"So that is your wife, I suppose?" I ask, sure that her beauty and the situation perfectly match how I met my wife story.

"Nah, that was all business, kid. We met a handful of times while in business together, but I was young when I made that deal. I was, I think, 30 at the time, plus I have a thousand more stories like that. For instance, take Ibiza, Spain...."

The old man puts his Sazerac down on the saucer and leans in as if the following story holds a lot more weight.

"Ibiza is the land of opportunity if you are a sexual deviant; drugs, women, music, nude beaches, clubs, yacht parties; the nights never seem to end."

The old man points at my drink, motioning for me to take another sip, but I'm back down to a quarter left on my second glass, so I put it back down on my saucer plate. I have taken his warning about the four drinks very seriously, so I know I need to slow it down while the old man tells this next story.

"I've heard many stories about Ibiza, but I've never been." I shake my head and shrug my shoulders. "I hear it is fucking bananas. Like parties every day, crazy house music, sex...." He waves his hand in the air

"Let me finish."

A reminiscent smile makes his white goat tee glow in the bar lighting.

"Ibiza was a celebration after some colleagues and I started a tech company. Of course, going global for any company is a big fucking deal and a lot of work; needless to say, we were ready for some partying. I had just become a millionaire, and let me tell you, we went all out. I'm talking about yachts. We rented out a mansion at the top of the mountain, every club on the island was our playground, and the sea of women was something to make Zeus's envy spark fire throughout the universe."

I watch the old man, smiling, excited for him to continue.

"Describing the party beast that is Ibiza will not do it proper justice; you have to be there, you have to feel the music, smell the sweat, and hear the love."

The old man has a way of using his onyx-colored eyes to put extra enthusiasm into every word he uses. Eye pops, blinks of the eyelids, winks; it's as though his eyes attribute his diction.

"For ten nights, we ran wild. We brought about fifteen American women with us for some reason, but we didn't need to. On the first night, I decided to dabble with drugs for the first time."

The old man takes his right hand and wipes his face, attempting to wipe away some of the past chagrin.

"Before then, you never partook in any drug? You never smoked weed?" I ask the question curious, hoping that being a 'square' is not the secret to success.

"Come on, young blood, weed? Weeds are not a drug; you've got to know that."

The old man smacks me on the right knee, and we both laugh.

"So, what did you take?"

Once again, the old man shakes his head in disbelief of a night he had way back when.

"I took one of those ecstasy pills."

I ball my left hand into a fist and then laugh into it.

"Ha, Ha… No way you; you took an 'e' pill?"

The old man nods his head in embarrassment as though it was the most wonderfully terrible idea he ever had. Ecstasy is a crazy beast, and I imagine this old man's first experience was nothing short of fantastic.

"Let me just say you kids are crazy for doing that shit."

Onyx connects to the excitement of onyx, genuinely emphasizing the moment.

"I took that pill, and let me tell you, the "game" was times a hundred that night. I remember meeting two Norwegian women who were amazed by what they called "chocolate skin."

My gaze is locked on the old man. I have never seen a Norwegian woman in person, but damn, I sure would like to.

"They actually couldn't stop talking about my skin tone. We met at a club called Amnesia, of Fantasy, something like that, but it was the first time in my long life that I had a white person envious of my skin."

The old man gives me a stare, almost putting me in the moment with him. As a black man, it is always a shock when you meet white folks who love your skin color; it can catch you off guard.

"What was the name of that club?" He looks up to the roof for the name of the club. "I don't remember the name, either way, at this place…." The old man leans in, playfully smacking the outside of my right knee, bearing the grin of a dirty uncle.

"Let me tell you, everyone, I mean everyone, including the women, all of us, and I mean all of us; we were shirtless and ready—kissing and on the verge of the full monty."

The old man's accent seemed to be a mix of something southern, lodged with hints of Europe all over it, almost English—like he might end with a mate or something British at any moment. Even how he pronounces Ibiza seems to be an accent I've never heard. "A-bee-fa" is his pronunciation.

"So I am on the dancefloor getting it like I never have before. I'm telling you I've got moves, boy. Woo!" The old man claps his hands loudly. "I must have locked lips with twenty women, if not thirty. Man, that pill had me feeling like I never have before. Then I see these two white angels walking towards me." The old man reaches his arms out to receive them. "They both had perfect fucking breasts. I felt like two statues of Aphrodite had come to life just for me. And when I say perfect, boy, I mean perfect" The old man uses both of his hands cupped just under his chest to mimic how perky they were.

"No way. I've never seen a Norwegian woman, but oh my god."

My onyx drip from excitement; I am on the edge of my seat, yearning for more.

"What did they look like?"

My words come out anxious, hoping his description will wet my imagination.

"Hair so blonde, it looks white, eyes were moon mountain sapphire; they have a way of using their eyes to visualize your arousal, then go after it; skin like snow, but pink at the touch. Oh, and tall; these girls were stout." The old man grabs his Sazerac, takes a quick sip, then turns back to me.

"Anyway, I suppose these two Norwegian girls were tired of watching me float around the dance floor, kissing everyone…." The old man chuckles, "they decided that it was time that they too had a taste of chocolate." He clicks his tongue as though that's just how the game rolls. "My first of many threesomes and that might I add, was the first night. Night two, there was the crazy-ass girl from Spain who decided it was her duty to fuck me in as many public places as possible. Even McDonalds. Night three, we popped bottles at the biggest club I have ever seen. Sparklers, cocktail waitresses, big ass bottles, we were showing out. Shit, I think someone even blew fire at our table." The old man's body shakes with laughter as my jaw drops. "Well, it caught the attention of a certain princess whose name I can not mention. On the fourth night, one of the women we brought thought that maybe it was time for her to uh…."

He motions the sexual act using his hand, making his right hand into a circle, then using the left index figure to go in and out of the hole.

"And, of course, you did, right?"

"Fuck, no!" My shocked brow sends a slight pause as the old man continues.

"I told her that I didn't come all of the ways to Ibiza to sleep with an American girl, and then I walked off. That night I slept with three girls from Hungary, boozed up, coked-up, having the time of my fucking life. One particular Hungarian girl made my dick disappear while she sucked me off." The old man's words add gravity to my jaw.

"She deep throa...."

The old man nods his head while interrupting me.

"She deep throated all of me. Yes! I could go on about the other nights, but then you would just drool all over the bar, young buck."

The old man pauses for a second while I pick my jaw up off the floor.

"Order another drink." As the old man continues his story, he instructs me so I get Braxton's attention.

Braxton comes back over to begin the now familiar Sazerac ritual. "Yeah, I've had the opportunity to go to many places, meet many women, and kiss many faces. My boys would call it "globetrotting," and man was it a show."

The old man boasts as I await my third Sazerac. I watch that magical elixir shrink the sugar cube and then look back at the old man.

"From Vegas to France, Rome to Asia, and even "down under." I've met and bedded some of the most beautiful women in the world." The old man speaks as Braxton continues; three dashes of Peychaud's, three bits of angostura, rye whiskey, cognac.

"Each time I landed somewhere, my mission was the same. Meet a woman from the city, have fun with her, then on to the next one. Brazil, Hawaii, Russia, and even Alaska. The money will bring you lots of lust, young buck, but it won't bring you, love."

The last thing he says distracts me from the absinthe wash. I look at the old man, concerned.

"What do you mean?" I look over to the old man, giving him my undivided attention.

"It sounds like you had a hell of a time. It sounds like you were a fucking rock star. So what's this talk of love shit?" I ask, shocked as Braxton slides me my Sazerac.

"Do you know why I had you close your eyes and describe your girl Illegra?" The old man asks.

"I figure that you just love women enough to hear about them, probably the same reason you are here on a Friday night, looking at women." I retort with a chuckle.

"No. I wanted you to feel her; I wanted you to notice your love; I wanted you to smell and taste Illegra... Hey kid, did you notice what all of the women in my story had in common?" I shake my head.

"No names, no faces, nothing truly memorable besides a night of heavy breathing, the city I was in, and the drugs I took whilst being with them." I nod, understanding his sentiment.

"But you remembered Aurora; you knew what she looked like and everything," I say jokingly, giving the old man a knee tap.

"Aye.."

The old man grabs his glass to toast my clever remark.

"I definitely remember Aurora."

We share a laugh.

Chapter 7: The Moon Library

As the Sazerac begins to run through me, I fight the urge for that

much-needed release; a piss. Listening to the old man's stories has kept me from

breaking the seal; his words are so engaging that I have ignored the sting in my

bladder. Still, I can't remember the last time I was involved with such great

conversation. Sure we talk when I'm with the boys, but we never really

converse. I suppose there may be no difference between those who talk and those who converse in other circles, but there is more in my conversation with the old man than anything the boys and I have ever said.

The boys and I talk about the girls we have slept with, the girls we would like to sleep with, and often we speak of the girls we wouldn't sleep with, but we never converse. The boys and I speak of the old men and their prostitutes; we gawk at the waitresses in their skimpy outfits, making passes. And so often spend time clowning on each other's failed attempts, but we never genuinely talk or have anything of substance to say. Of course, the boys and I also speak of sports and current events, but this is not just speaking; we are conversing. With the old man, this is something entirely different.

Sure the old man spoke of his sexcapades, and Ibiza must have been one hell of a time, but his thoughts on love stuck like syrup to the walls of my mind. There was this subtle remorse in his stare, this longing, this regret. The old man said that he could never visualize his one true love, which plagues him somehow. The boys and I never have to visualize anyone; we are young; life is ahead, not behind, so why let the sad stare of a rich man play on my empathy?

If this were any other night, the boys and I would be plotting more mischievous accords—we wouldn't be talking of love. So what do we know of the myth that is love? Why think of what hasn't happened when there is so much life to live? I assume getting older will always make you feel for days past and months that have slipped away, but the boys and I are young men; love will always be there.

Thinking of the boys and our antics, I wonder where they might be and why they are not here. Looking around this bar, I see many faces, but not one that I truly recognize. On a typical Friday night, the boys and I would be a few shots deep by now; assuredly, we would be sharing our hands at interactions and rejections from any number of women, and with liquid courage serving as sword and shield. We are fools like that, leaping through a life of booze, babes, and bad ideas. But still, this old man is too engaging for normal reactions, and I suppose that this moment has happened the way it has because it has to be.

The captivating cadence of the old man's words has blurred the night and the faces around, stealing my attention. This combination of great stories and Sazeracs has a hypnotizing elegance that I've never played a part in before this night. The assiduity that I've shown the old man has turned my local "watering hole" foreign, so foreign that the only person I recognize most in this godforsaken place is that smug fucker Chris.

Looking at Chris as my body speaks in a twist of my bladder, alerting me it is time to hit the head, I know a journey to the bathroom is a must, plus it will give me time away from the old man so that I can check the place out.

"I'll be right back, old buck."

I tease the old man before taking a swig of my Sazerac. I place my Sazerac back on the saucer leaving the glass half-empty.

"Ok young blood; I suppose you need to hit the pisser?"

I nod while pushing my stool out, and the old man continues.

"Yeah, the Sazerac will run through you like that, but the twist of the bladder is only the beginning. Have any questions arise in your head? Has the mind begun to stir?" The sound of the old man's harmonic warning chills my nerves.

"Questions? No questions, old buck, just have to pee," I reply side-eye as I get up from my seat.

Why have I lied to the old man? There have been many questions, and the mind stirs more than any cocktail in this place, but still, I lie.

"Yeah," the old man looks at me with a side-eye, holding his Sazerac in his left hand, "I bet."

He sizes me up from head to toe, then back up as onyx connects to onyx.

"No worries, young man, I'll make sure that no old fuckers take your "seat.'"

The old man teases quotations in the air, chuckling as I slide past him.

"Ha, Ha. Please do; I'd hate to have another confrontation with one of our elderly citizens."

I playfully tap the old man on the back, then stretch my arms.

While stretching my arms, I look in the bathroom's direction, through the stadium seating, up a few stairs, then to the left of the tufted sofas. Although the bathroom down here is obviously closer, I see that smug fucker Chris and his crew.

Viewing Chris's crew and his women, the appeal of the upstairs bathroom begins to warm my bladder, but I'm mindful that my detour will not be a hasty retreat. The staircase leading upstairs is located on the other side of the bar, on the building's left corner from where I sit. A mahogany staircase leads up into an area aptly named "Moon library." This winding staircase drops down into the stadium seating, leading up to a librarian's Valhalla.

Visualizing my path, I will have to make my way through slutty girls, drunk fellas, and raging cocktail waitresses to hit the bathroom upstairs. It is a daunting journey, but I prefer this route over any encounter with that flash fucker Chris, so I begin my stroll.

Even more crowded than I expected, I began regretting my real rivalry with Chris; nevertheless, I can not ignore this pee. Undoubtedly, there will be a few bumps along the way; the "Rum" resembles more of a club than a bar; I continue fighting through.

The entire vibe of this place has the rowdy intent of a Sin City nightclub with so many people doing so many nonsensical things. Maybe the old man is right; perhaps the Sazerac is stirring my brain? Some things that I have never noticed now seem so apparent on this peculiar Friday night. Walking around the oval bar area towards the serpentine stairs, I see many faces doing many things. I hear the voices and chit-chat as though I am a part of every conversation. As if time were of my possession, I move through the crowd as an avatar of observation, using my onyx to survey the night.

I see the novice waving a twenty in the air, hoping to get a quick drink, but to no avail. Next, I spot the bachelorette group that has just arrived, who have more than likely come from a strip club or some sort of Chippendale's situation. These women look anxious to end the night right—mingling with guys, taking shots, desperate for attention. Then there are the men on the hunt. These big, burly brothas pounce on every woman passing them by. They push breath threw teeth, whistle; they grab at women.

"Chit, chit... Aye, gurl!"

Their catcalls seem more than degrading, something so cheap about their approach; they look so starved, like vultures pecking for scraps. At least the boys and I never do that—clawing at women like dogs off lease. The boys and I take more pride in our advances, creating genuine conversation; we would never refer to such barbaric outbursts—sounding like horned out animals. The ebony men give me competitive looks and eye rolls as I walk by, looking as though my very presence has threatened their "game."

Observing these fools makes me realize the boys and I are too refined for such behavior—such foolish competition. Sure we have our player tendencies, and we all love women, but we approach our ladies with more respect; the boys and I are more refined than these clowns. It makes me laugh, thinking the word refined has no place in describing the "boys," but this concept works just fine compared to these doltish brothas.

Viewing all of these faces and bodies, doing whatever they can to be seen, makes me wonder; where exactly do I belong in the mix of all this?

I continue walking in the direction of the twisting mahogany staircase, then notice the massive skylight. I look up to it as I walk, hoping the milk stream will offer some much-needed answers to these developing questions. This giant window gives a clear view of the moon on most nights, and tonight, there is a beautiful full moon looking down into the "Rum." With the lights dimmed, a vanilla stream shoots down into this place like the great word of God. The "Moon Library" always holds a specific incantation, but it feels like so much more tonight.

How marvelous is the moon? What magic does it have to control waves, provide light, and change the beat of a heart?

The upstairs bodies seem like floating silhouettes, dancing, moving in a trance, and the moon is bright. Enchantment feels my stomach—something more potent than the twist of my bladder, something more enchanting than monotonous chatter.

Have I never seen the moon before tonight? Have I ever let the lunar energy take hold of my being?

My hand cascades on the railing as I ascend into the Moon Library, finding myself in awe of lunar majesty. Without the mahogany banister to guide me, I would be lost—I would be captured in the magic of the moon, this sudden magnetism that I've never felt before, pulling me, coercing me into thought.

The full moon's enticement at this moment can only be described as the seductive universe taking hold of nighttime desire. The moon always has a way of arousing provocative energy, and the "Rum" is the perfect place for all of it; such a fantastic setting for a fabulous bar.

Often I enjoy taking the scenic route around any place I attend, checking things out, getting "a lay of the land," feeling like a lion stalking his territory—letting others know that I am around. I have always been curious about what people are getting into; the laughter, the snide looks, forged happiness; the signs that most people can't read are those I notice most.

Perhaps it is FOMO (fear of missing out); my brain is nosy like that; always wanting to know all of what goes on, always watching, always listening, always making sure I know the ends and outs of any situation.

Looking at all of the beautiful women in this place is nice, but as I look, I notice that not one of these attention-hoarding girls can hold a candle to "Leggy." Illegra is much more than a pretty face and saucy attitude, she is way more interesting than any of these girls, and her beauty is marvelous. The shine of her black hair. That walk. Those lips. For a split second, I can smell her. The aroma of Illegra is like the smell of the clouds in heaven, an inviting fragrance—the authentic scent of home.

Reaching the top of the mahogany stairs, I notice a beautiful girl as she begins to laugh. I take a right around the top banister into the first seating area. The "Moon Library" upstairs design is identical on both ends, except the bathroom can be found in the far left corner from where I stand. The seating area across from me is more intimate than this area; candles and more oversized sofas look like a vampire's favorite seat.

The long walkway connecting both ends has more books, couples seating, and more books, looking like the magnificent walkway of an ancient athenaeum. All couches and chairs are made of luxurious, obsidian leather, accentuated by stained golden buttons. These tufted couches and chairs look so decedent, fit for kings and queens, but drunken dullards have taken place.

The exterior is forged of bookshelves; massive walls of leather-bound books that smell so new. It seems as though knowledge holds this impressive structure together. Then there is mahogany and obsidian railing. The railing forms the barrier, the most elegant safety protocol one's eyes could ever see. This gating is fashioned in this gothic-victorian design, suiting the entire building like a belt would complete a luxurious ensemble.

As I turn my attention back to the walkway, the girl begins to laugh. The buzz in my ear is so noxious that I find myself becoming slightly annoyed. The way her laugh sits inside my ears—this vexatious cackle, I feel my ears might bleed. My head shakes unattracted, feeling sorry for those around me.

As I continue walking into the seating area, I spot another dark-haired beauty at the end, sitting by a bookshelf. The girl holds her phone up in the air, puckering her lips, ignoring all those around her. She attempts to find the perfect picture, the ideal angle, waving people out of the way, cursing those who dare interrupt the process. She is so into herself, so vain, the conceit of this woman is so appalling, I have to look away.

Heading down the walkway, viewing all of these faces that sit around, the people taking pictures, performing selfies. These damn selfies have to be the newest fad clawing at my last nerve. It is such a turn-off seeing a woman so into herself, so unengaging. "Leggy" is nothing like these silly girls with their phones; she has more.

"Leggy" never does such things as take selfies, excluding herself from the crowd. Instead, "Leggy" takes silly pictures; she "photobombs," and she's so animated in everything she does. Illegra is fun, fun and hilarious, and more gorgeous than any of these foolish girls. It makes me laugh, thinking of how funny she is. Illegra has this effortless humor about her, and if a joke is extra amusing, you might just get a snort out of her—a snort which is even more hilarious than any jape. Her laugh has a subtle innocence. So very genuine, like adolescent tittering, which creates a smile that always steals me; hell, "Leggy's" smile does more than stop traffic on most days. Her smile controls heartbeats. It warms and tickles me. Illegra's teeth are so white and big when she smiles, a shine worthy of molding souls. "Leggy" is open and friendly, loving, and understanding.

"Leggy," my Illegra is a woman that makes all of these women seem so counterfeit in comparison.

Getting past the selfie shoots, I take a closer look at the bookshelves. They seem to be fifteen-twenty feet high, with large mahogany bookshelves that reach the top of the Victorian ceiling—helping to hold this God-like structure in place.

Like everything in the "Rum," the bookshelves have spared no expense. The wood shines like the coat of a freshly groomed stallion, a deep shine that reflects light as I look.

Walking around, I wonder if I have ever genuinely taken a look at the elegance of the "Moon Library?" Have I ever been upstairs before this time? I have been to the "Rum" hundreds of times before, but I've never noticed this.

How is it that I have missed all of the details in this place? How have I missed the rich burgundy tone of the bookshelves glowing in the vanilla stream?

It feels as though I have entered a royal library of some ancient Czar, as though Zeus himself provided the designs of this magnificent Library. The ceiling has been painted in this intricate design; I imagine Michael Angelo must have been resurrected just to create such masterful artwork. Murals of angels in every skin tone and all different races, sizes, and shapes reach each other. I grab the mahogany balustrade with black victorian gating that forms a half-moon design built over top of the bar. Looking down at the coliseum-style bar, I feel like I am on a balcony of some grand theater. All of the movement downstairs provides the perfect show for the onyx of observation. It is theater, is it not? The night's activities; cocktail waitresses race from end to end with drinks and money, bartenders provide excitement with flair, and the people; so many people.

Looking down, I am starting to realize that I'm just a part of the show on most nights, not really standing out in any way, blending in with the norm of single life. I look for a moment more, becoming disappointed with my normality.

This quick loathsome moment makes me turn away from the balustrade, continuing down the path to the bathroom. I notice how the bookshelves line up all around the top floor, as though the owner decided that bookshelves instead of traditional walls would be more suitable to hold up the magnificent ceiling. There is this rich smell of unleafed books, mahogany, and lavender. Something so distinguished about this entire top floor, this smell, like the aroma is part of the ventilation, somehow pumped into the air. Even with all of the bodies around, the "Moon Library" smells much different from downstairs; it feels like an entirely different venue.

Although the first seating area is the best place to take advantage of the massive skylight, I can still feel the energy as I walk through. The window resembles a giant eye looking right up into the moon, and the light shines so bright and so proud that I can feel the moonbeam on my back as I stroll toward the bathroom. I take a look back to gaze up into the large window. The skylight is massive and clear; no spots, smudges, or stains. I feel as though I am outside, unbothered, alone with just the universe for a split second.

I wonder if the universe knows how beautiful the night sky is and how mesmerizing her presence can be? The glass is so clear, and the moon is so beautiful. It's like a massive contact lens placed on the "Rum" for a clear view of the night. The catty-corner placement makes the moon shine bright as the "bat signal," as a floodlight—I feel the energy of the moonlight, beginning to embrace what it all might mean fully; the lunar energy feels so visceral, almost buoyant within the "Rum."

Maybe the Sazerac is stirring the mind and asking questions?

As I continue walking, I notice a redhead surrounded by men. The guys look like battling auctioneers fighting for the redhead's attention. These men are so hard pressed, like cocks fighting for a hen, I wonder if they have even noticed where they stand. They are so focused on the redhead instead of genuinely enjoying the bar, instead of enjoying moonlight as it shines into the Library. Men are such fools in the presence of beauty; this exercise of archaic rivalry that most men suffer.

The men tell off-kilter jokes, and the redhead vaguely laughs. The redhead seems barely amused at the scene, watching two men who never have a chance to fight for her attention. Illegra never needs such attention; she shies away from such things.

The first night I met Illegra, she was on the dancefloor with her girls, enjoying herself. She cared not about the men around or the free drinks that could be had; she was dancing because she loved the music; it was fun for her. The only way I stole her attention was by dancing. I have to credit my moves for that night; otherwise, I would have never received the beautiful Illegra as I did.

Observing the bar from this newfound bird's eye view, noticing these parts of life, questioning my place, I wonder if this was all worth it?. These women and men fighting for the attention of their self-involved counterparts all seem so forced, like clones fucking. There is this counterfeit nature to dating life, these people, and this night. It all seems so beneath what I already have and should appreciate more. For the first time, I begin to notice how flawed this scene is; all of the bar scene's flaws have finally come to the surface; mine included.

I get to the bathroom door as a drunken fool stumbles out. I sway to the left, letting his inebriation slide by without a shoulder check. I'm feeling a little more than tipsy by this time, but damn, I feel great.

What is this old fucker making me drink?

It is a different kind of drunk than I have ever felt, more high than intoxicated. I think I am floating through the "Rum," walking on air. This shit is damn good—I am on this coherent cloud of intoxication, and each vibration seems to fuel my mind. Everything seems more defined; I'm looking at the world more in-depth, with this abundance of nuance.

I have always seen the world through a more profound lens than those appointed, but now I'm thinking like never before. Somehow I feel like my senses have dialed in more on the feel than just the sight. Alcohol usually has this heavy feeling in the stomach, but this Sazerac seems to vibrate at a completely different frequency. I push through the mahogany door of the bathroom.

As is everything in the "Rum," the bathroom is dressed in gorgeous auburn wood. You can almost smell its purity, but the miasma masculinity clouds the fragrance.

Each stall is mahogany. The dividers between the urinals are mahogany; even the frames around the mirrors are all mahogany—a deep burgundy compliments the black tile—given a rustic obeisance that brings together the entire decor.

How much did this fucking place cost? The tile on the floor is expensive; every other square is black marble, each with an ivory accent that resembles veins—veins of a living, breathing castle of debauchery and hopeful frolics. This decor is unique, and then my body reminds me of why I entered.

I walk past the sinks; a black tiled wall separates the bathroom stalls and urinals from the handwashing fixtures as you walk in, so I walk past the obsidian divider. The stalls are on the left and the urinals to the right. I pick the last urinal, and nobody seems to be in either stall.

"Aaaah!!!"

The release shuts my eyes, putting me in a momentary daze. Sometimes breaking the seal feels better than the liquor going down. I lean my head back, looking up at the roof, feeling like it might be the best piss I have ever had.

BOOM!!

Someone kicks the door open, obviously drunk. I can hear him walk into the bathroom, stumbling through, stomping on the floor tile. As the drunk kid walks around to the urinals, I quickly look at his disheveled features, desperately avoiding eye contact.

"Hey, Hey, Rastaman!" The drunken fool says as he picks the urinal right next to me.

I place my face forward, looking at the black tile. There are five other open urinals to my right, but the dullard chooses the one next to me.

"How goes the night, rastaman? "

The drunken frat boy burns my left temple with his gaze. His energy is circular; his balance is off.

"It's a good night. Can't really complain."

I quickly say, being polite and ending the brief interaction by looking at the tile as I pee. The release feels good; I am almost mad at the dullard's interruption. Hoping to avoid further communication, I push out all of the Sazerac and beer as fast as possible.

After I flush, I walk to the sinks to wash my hand, and then he says one last thing.

"Hey, rastaman, bro, do you have some, bud?"

The drunken fool lets out a stoner chuckle. I look back at him with a smirk. I have to admit the guy is one of those harmless drunks, like the slapstick winos of yesteryear; he means well, and the little bit of hilarity in his voice deserves a reply.

"I wish. Ha, but I'm sure someone else does." I say before walking to wash my hands. I wash my hands quickly, using a paper towel to dry each hand before leaving.

I'm not even sure that I could smoke herb right now with how I feel on this Sazerac. I'm not quite drunk, but not sober; no slurred words, but my vision is slightly clouded; it feels like I'm in a Prince video.

Walking around has done me some good; hell seeing the crowd has done me some good; I guess it's as the old man said, "the Sazerac stirs the mind."

I walk over to the balustrade. I place both hands on it, grabbing hold of the mahogany. I stand for a moment to observe the bar from a birds-eye view again, drinking it all in.

The people below remind me of crabs in a crate from this height. All clawing at each other, all are trying so hard for attention. They are like caged animals, not in their primal element but trying to put on this not entirely natural act. It is a movement that might just attract an audience, so they continue. It feels so sad, so forced. I release the balustrade and make my way through the upstairs crowd heading back to the spiral staircase.

Man, I feel different. A smile develops on my face, my skin feels like a slight breeze has hit, goosebumps form from excitement, and my vision has the sight of each vibration that moves throughout the bar. It feels almost psychedelic, and I'm making my way down the spiral staircase before I know it.

Did taking a piss enhance my intoxication?

As I'm thinking of my trip, right before I reach the last step, I peer at the front door spotting my boy Dee as he walks in. Oh shit, I forgot I don't have my phone; he must have been trying to get ahold of me. The remainder of what I might have missed sends a spark through me as I rush toward Dee.

Dee walks down to the front part of the bar closest to the entrance; I stealth the crowd making sure he doesn't see me as I approach.

Typically Dee comes to the "Rum" dressed to the nines, with some fancy cologne and clean fade. He is a light-skinned brotha, about 6'2", compared continuously to Michael Ealy. Admittedly Dee is a good-looking kid, and his peridot eyes make most girls swoon.

Dee has always been the one in our crew that women flock to; most nights, he gets precisely the woman he wants and always dresses so fresh. Tonight Dee is in a baseball cap and a hoodie, looking like a person trying to hide from the crowd; very incognito.

"Yo nigga…" I sneak up on Dee, tapping him on the shoulder. "What up?" The bass of my voice rings his ear.

"Oh shit, Malic, where the fuck you come from?" Dee asks as he looks around, not too concerned with my answer. "Did you just get here?" He asks, almost as if I am bothering him, then looks over to the bartender as though he can't wait to get her attention.

"Nah, I was in the bathroom upstairs; I've been here for a minute," I answer while Dee looks uninterested, almost preoccupied. He keeps looking towards the bar anxiously.

"I forgot my phone at the house, so I wasn't able to see if you and Alex were coming out tonight, so I just figured…."

I look around for Alex but don't see him walking in or around anywhere. We are usually linked up together, prowling the town, searching for trouble, booty, or both.

"Where's that nigga Alex at?" I ask, knowing that Alex can't be far behind. The three of us are like peas in a pod, so it is weird not to see at least two of us together.

"Yeah, we had been texting your ass all night long, so we figured you were locked up with your girl…." His tone is meant to tease me, knowing that Illegra and I are not boyfriend and girlfriend. "I mean, Illegra." Dee laughs as I playfully push him.

"But fa' real where dat nigga Alex at?" I ask.

It is funny how I get around Dee, then automatically start talking like some damn rap artist when moments ago, with the old man, I attempted the diction of a Harvard graduate.

"He's out on a date with that girl from last week; remember the blonde with the fake tits?" Dee says with a tiny tickle in his throat; I nod my head in a confusing yes like I remember but only half remember.

"Yeah, I remember, the one that kinda looks like a "Baywatch" blonde from the 90s.." Dee points to me, laughing and nodding his head.

"Well, apparently, they have hit it off pretty damn good. They've spent the entire week together." Dee then put both of his hands up, shrugging his shoulders in this sort of "I don't know" motion before waving a bartender over that has a bag of packaged food.

"No shit," I say, surprised.

"Mister "I don't need more than one night with a woman" has spent a week with someone?" I shake my head in disbelief at Alex's uncharacteristic actions. Dee gives me a smirk and a nod.

Dee is half looking at me, half-turned trying to get the bartender's attention as she makes her way over from the other side.

"How much do I owe you?"

Dee yells out to the bartender, then grabs his wallet from his back right pocket.

"I was surprised by it myself, that fucking kid," Dee says before squeezing in between two patrons as he grabs the check presenter from the bartender.

These two people look irritated by Dee's movement. They crowd the bar, so they shouldn't be looking at Dee like that, but it is a pretty crowded area.

"And what's going on here?" I say, pointing at his bag of food on the bar as he ruffles through to make sure all that he ordered is there. Once again, the two patrons look kind of irritated and impatient.

"You don't have to look at me like I'm ruining your night…Let me just get my food and my check, and then I'll be out of here."

Dee snaps at the patrons and then takes one last check before grabbing the two bags off the bar and holding them in his right hand.

"Well, I'm having a "Netflix and chill" night with that nurse I met about a month ago."

Dee gives me an in-depth look as if it will help me remember one of the many girls he has come across. He then places his credit card in the check presenter and hands it to the bartender. Dee gives the two patrons crowding the bar another death stare. They look back at him equally as deadly.

"Nurse?" I say, confused, grabbing his attention, feeling betrayed somehow.

"What nurse?" I ask with urgency as though he has been lying to me.

"Damn, you don't remember any woman unless she has colored eyes, black hair, and long legs." Dee teases me once again about Illegra.

"Remember when we went bowling, then I ran away towards the bathroom, missing my turn?" Dee has his left hand on my right shoulder, trying to implant the night in my head.

"Yeah, I remember you holding our fucking game up.." Dee releases my shoulder and gives me a kind of "You got it" pat.

"That's this girl." He ends up excited with a Herculean grin as he hurries back into the bar to receive his check.

"Thank you, sweety!"

Dee says to the bartender, who places the check presenter on the bar between the two patrons for Dee to sign. They look at him yet again, but he ignores them while switching the bags over to his left, grabs the pen with his right, then skillfully signs and tips with one hand.

"I'm sorry to inconvenience you in such a way. I hope I didn't ruin your night." He snaps at the patrons with some much-deserved snark, then shakes his head in utter disgust.

"Nice mustache!" Dee says to the female patron before stepping away from the bar.

The woman holds her right hand over her top lip; the man with the woman looks like he wants to say something to Dee but then begins searching the woman's face for facial hair.

I stand shocked, not because of the two patrons but surprised as my boys have both ended up with their own women tonight. My boys spend their fucking nights on dates while I'm virtually alone at the bar. I begin to feel foolish, as I have obviously missed the memo or some shit. Dee veers toward the entrance.

"Are you here alone? You look a little twisted." Dee asks with a concerned tone, stopping, then Peridot connects to onyx.

"No, I'm actually over at my spot kicking it with this cool-ass old dude. He is rich as fuck," I say excitedly, hiding the shameful fact that I did come alone. "Come over and meet this cat."

I start to lead him over to the spot, and Dee reluctantly follows me. "Look, he is over here in my seat." We both look to see that no one is sitting there.

"I don't see anybody, kid, plus I got to get back to Vanessa. She's in the car waiting." He pulls away from me, walking toward the entrance; I follow him to the door.

"O, so this "nurse" has a name?"

I ask, mimicking quotation marks to mock him. Dee nods, hiding a smile. Although he smirks, his eyes look frustrated at my possible intoxication. I seem to be holding him up, so I decide to let him be.

"Well damn, brotha, alright, have a good night," I say, confused with some weird hint of defeat in my voice.

Dee puts both bags in his left hand, then places his right hand on my shoulder one more time with the Peridot of concern. We stand just before the entrance.

People pass behind him, coming in and out, all of these faces coming and going. The drunk switch out with the sober, some women leaving get replaced by fellas coming; Dee's peridot sends worry to my onyx, looking as though they want to tell me something—as though I need to hear something valuable about myself. They are caring eyes, but then something holds them back. Whatever he wanted to say, the gleam in his peridot tells me that tonight will not be the night his words take form.

"Yo, take care of yourself, Malic. And don't get too twisted." We give each other a brotherly hug before he heads out of the massive mahogany doors. I look at him as he walks away, feeling the energy of honest words not said.

Dee has a date, Alex sounds like he is falling in love, and I'm at the "Rum" drinking with an old man. For the third time tonight, I feel like a fool.

I step back away from the entrance, people are passing me in and out, but I feel nothing. I decide to go around the bar gandering at the massive skylight as I walk past crowds of people. Sluggishly I walk through the crowd, stupefied by who I am becoming and how this night has turned out.

What am I doing here when I have a beautiful woman at home? What is going on in my head that makes me so damn foolish? What sign do I need to recognize what I've got?

What do I want out of life?

As my mind stirs and the real question arises, I hear the old man's voice."The second Sazerac asks a question, a question that many never want to ask."

Once I am below the skylight, I look up as people pass, and the night continues. I look up into the massive skylight viewing the moon, feeling the moon, hoping to hear the moon.

Will the moon please give me some answers? Will the stars shine some sense into me?

I stand looking up into the skylight, hopeful that the moon and universe will hear my inner cry for clarity.

Chapter 8: Lone Wolf

Walking back around the bar, taking the turn in the direction of my seat, through the debaucherous crowd, past the catcalling black dudes, I find myself feeling confused and uncertain, and perhaps seeing Dee triggered this depressing float, or the Sazerac, or Illegra. Either way, I'm walking without a guide.

I'm on the end furthest from the entrance, on the way to my seat, feeling sorry for myself, then I lift my head. I spot the old man from a distance. He is looking into his drink, rotating the glass every so often. The old man turns the rock's glass round and round on the saucer dish, creating a vortex with the pinkish-brown liquid, contemplating things I dare not understand.

The old man looks into the Sazerac as though some untold answers lie within the magical elixir, within this vortex created by his developing melancholy. As I watch him from this distance, I notice that which I had not before seen; from where I stand, his loneliness is so apparent—a virtual ghost within the shadows. People revolve around him; he is in the middle of a party, yet nothing seems to phase him. Whereat first, I saw an old man too arrogant to be bothered; now, I see an elder statesman, alone in the time, perhaps alone in the world. He does not view the beautiful faces, he has no word for any bartender, and the old man hasn't looked up once to see if I am on my way back. Instead, he stares into his Sazerac, rotating it on the saucer as the liquor turns.

It is sad in a way, a man of that age, alone at the bar, perhaps alone in the world. My head shakes in sadness as it occurs to me that the old man's life might not be all I believe it is cracked up to be; some eggs are yoked, others can be dead chickens. But, realizing there might be a deeper reason for him being alone tonight—there must be some other purpose behind our newfound friendship, I begin to warm up to the idea of comforting this old, lonely man.

I wonder if the old man has a family or if he has ever been married? I wonder if he has kids that have kids, or even great-grandkids? I wonder if he has friends and those friends have kids, and how their families all get along? I wonder if he has ever visualized a woman in how he made me visualize Illegra? Has this man ever known love? I wonder where he goes after this and what waits for the old man after the Sazerac runs out?

I decide I must find out more about this man, so I head back to my seat.

"Did you fall in, young buck, or has the Sazerac gotten a hold of ya? Ha, Ha."

The old man playfully pats me on the right side of my back with his left hand. I can feel the strength of years with each pat, but it is not painful, more endearing, like mini hugs from a grandfather.

I sit down next to the old man with a slight smirk on my face, but his little joke could never rectify what I have just witnessed. Perhaps he could feel my mood as I walked up and wanted to lighten the air, but seeing him alone, as he was before I sat, has created an empathetic curiosity. I grab my Sazerac, then take a long, slow sip.

"Aah."

The old man gives me a concerned look.

"Are you doing ok young buck? What happened in that bathroom?"

I put the glass back down on the saucer and then look over to the old man.

"Nothing happened, just the anatomy of a drinker. Also, I ran into one of my boys; I was going to bring him over, but you were nowhere to be found. Where'd you go?"

I ask with a curious look.

"Well, unlike you, young man, I wasn't going to fight those stairs...." The old man chuckles while pointing in the direction of the spiral staircase

"The moon library is a beautiful sight, but there happens to be a perfectly good restroom behind us, up over there by your good "friend" Chris."

We both turn our stools around; the old man points toward the bathroom as though he is showing me something new. The sarcasm of his elder humor seems to entertain him, so I play along.

"I'll tell you what, that boy still appears to be more intrigued with you than any women around. Are you sure he doesn't have a thing for you?"

Like some weird enchantment of rivalry, Chris glances over at me. Hazel connects to onyx, and I quickly turn to face the bar. The old man teases me more about Chris; I brush off his remarks with head nods, and Sazerac sips.

"Yeah, Yeah…"

I slightly giggle, thinking I want to get past the jokes and ask about his family, or lack thereof. I'd like to know why a sixty, seventy, or even eighty-something-year-old man finds himself at a single's bar on this Friday night. The old man seems to have it all together, yet, here he is. I look at the old man without words.

How do I ask him? How do I get even more personal than before? How do I justify bringing up what might be a painful past? And who am I to make such inquisitions?

"Why the long face, young buck?"

The old man inquires, intently looking at me before taking a sip of his Sazerac. I quickly say, "Nothing," before taking a sip of my Sazerac.

Maybe I am feeling sorrow for the old man? Perhaps I am frustrated that Chris keeps staring at me as though he is devising a plan? Maybe my face holds on to the frustration of possibly losing my "boys?" Or maybe, just perhaps, the realization that the end of my relationship is near, which paints the picture to be read?

The truth is I have no idea why the news of my "boys" having dates makes me feel so negative; hell, I've ditched the "boys" a time or two to stay in the warm embraces of "Leggy," yet I feel as though I've been given bad news. Shouldn't I be happier for my boys? And Chris, why should I even care about that silly fucker Chris?

Assuredly he has not a chance on the coldest day in hell to get "Leggy" back, but for some reason, I feel threatened by that fucker more than ever. I grind my teeth at the thought of him.

For a moment, I think about Chris about the "boys," Illegra, and then I think of the old man. The wheels in my brain are churning, this unlubricated grind that almost feels painful.

"Hey, where are your wife and kids? Where's your family?"

The words leap out of my mouth before I can catch them. I guess my brain just needed to know, or I needed to stop thinking about the "boys," Illegra, and that dullard Chris. The old man looks at me, shocked, taken back by my outburst of questions. He takes the half-empty glass of Sazerac into his left hand and does not put one eye on me as he pulls the glass to his lips. Not one eye, then he drinks.

"Aah.."

The old man puts his glass down on the saucer, looking out into the liquor shelf. I can tell that his life chapters are cycling through his brain, like an old library catalog, leafing through moments of his life. He looks at the liquor shelf, not viewing the bottles or the decor; he looks through the frame into the distant past.

I begin quietly observing the old man when his watch catches my eye yet again. The beautiful movements in the timepiece begin to put me in a trance, but then the old man speaks.

"As you can tell from tonight, young buck, I'm what some would call a "lone wolf" and have been for quite some time."

The old man takes another drink, probably his most enormous gulp of the night.

"Aah."

He holds the glass in both hands, looking deep into the liquid for all of his answers. The old man continues speaking to me whilst looking deep into the crystal rocks glass.

"Much like you, or almost exactly like you, I was foolishly ambitious. I was reckless and unwilling to realize the gifts before me. My ambition…"

The old man clicks his tongue between the roof of his mouth and his top teeth.

"My ambition has gotten me many trinkets, taken me many places, and brought me great wealth…."

He looks over to me.

"But wealth can't buy you everything. It certainly won't keep the things you hold most dear at bay, especially if you don't put in the work to keep them happy."

The old man places his Sazerac on the saucer dish, biting his lip, slightly shaking his head.

"No matter how great your wealth, true love will have a price that no amount of money can pay."

The old man states this with the most impactful tone, sounding as though this very well might be his most important lesson. It has amazed me how this man can hold my attention. The words he says, the looks, something about this old man intrigues me and has kept my intrigue, much like a favorite teacher or favorite uncle holding a child's attention.

"I would say you have great wealth. That watch might cost more than this entire place," I say, trying to lighten the old man's angst before he waves off my comment as if his wealth is no big deal.

"Yes, I have this watch and many, many more. I have a home in Italy, a large home in New York overlooking the park, a beach house in Fiji, and countless other homes worldwide. I have so many cars that I can't even count; An Aston Martin that would make Sean Connery swoon, a 67' Shelby, Mustang with an engine so loud it would shake the very foundation of this place like an earthquake. I have a few Maseratis, a limited edition Royce Royce SUV, a Tank, and many other cars in areas I can't even remember. I own 25 companies; Companies, not businesses, most of which have gone public. I'm worth close to 200 billion dollars and looking to make another 50 billion dollars this year alone. I will own a private island by the end of the year, I have two yachts and four planes, but do you know what I think about most?"

Onyx connects to onyx with the old man hoping that I know the answer. Instead, I just shake my head, mouth open in disbelief of all he owns.

How could I ever know the answer? How could someone like me ever hope to know the answers that a wealthy man seeks?

"I think about how all of the homes I own are empty; how nobody will drive my cars; I think if it was all worth having no "wolf pack" to call my own just to become a successful loner. I wonder if shutting myself off from the rest of the world was worth it."

He raises his glass to his mouth and takes a solemn sip.

"Aah.."

His pensive sip is followed by deep thought as he looks directly at me.

"For as long as I remember, I have been on my own."

The old man thinks back for a spell.

"You see, I didn't always have money, actually quite the opposite; no, I had to earn everything I had for myself. Raised by drug addicts, dirt poor, and when I was a kid, gangs, drug dealing, pimping, or robbing seemed to be the only options that people in my hood considered. For some reason, ebony folks tend to squander their talents claiming that life's limited options lead them to do bad things. It leads them to rob—it leads them to sell drugs to their people—it leads them down criminal pathways, unscrupulous behaviors, but I never believed in such loutish actions."

The education of each word resonates, and I couldn't agree more. I, too, came from a broken home, I also decided against criminal acts, and I, too, believe in much more than others do.

"No, rather than follow a pack of fools getting in trouble, I stayed alone with my books, ideas, and future plans to become the "lone wolf" that you see today."

The old man proudly states before taking a sip.

"Aah.."

The old man looks at me with the onyx of pride, yet I feel he has avoided my questions about marriage and family; still, I let him continue. He is getting closer to answering my questions; it's right there on the tip of his tongue.

"My family wasn't the Brady's, nor were my parents what you would call traditional. I never truly knew my father only spoke with him a handful of times, and my mother had a severe drug problem. I guess I can say I never truly knew her either."

As the old man speaks, I nod in agreement as I can relate to his sentiment. My father wasn't around for long; my mother was a drug addict, and my sister dated drug dealers and various deplorable individuals while she was a prostitute. I am a "Lone Wolf," I left home when I was fourteen and never looked back. So a lot of what the old man is explaining, I understand entirely, and for the first time tonight, I feel like his equal, well, at least in that regard.

I let the old man continue talking; hearing such similarities is inspiring. If this old man can grow into a billionaire from a shady past, then so can I. We finally relate much more than with drinks, even if the old man does not entirely know.

"So when I was in high school, once my mother's addiction became too intense, I had no choice but to leave. I had to grow up much faster than expected, unable to relate with any of my friends, unable to play sports, unable to enjoy the spoils of youth, so I took things into my own hands and never looked back. Growing up so fast, I began to work early; even my teachers were intimidated."

He then grabs his glass off the bar with his right hand, takes a sip, and I can see the horrors of his childhood hidden within the onyx. I hold the old man's sentiment, and I feel it is my turn to shed a little light on my dark past, come due. So, as the old man takes a sip of his Sazerac, I begin.

"I, too, came from not the most glamorous upbringing. My mother was a heroin addict, and my sister, well, my sister did what she had to do, I suppose."

There is something about the gems of those abused; it's a specific cloud we all see in each other, these dishonorable badges of unkind lives. My face falls for a moment, as I recall. I've become accustomed to holding such things in, almost blocking them out, but something so comforting in the old man's sorrow can be seen in his onyx. Who would imagine something so dark could be so comfortable? I have never told anyone about my childhood's horrors, but I feel a certain kinsmanship here and now with this old man.

A subtle relief comes over me as that honesty dribbles from my lips, like this weight I've been lugging around since childhood has finally lifted. Then onyx connects to onyx as we realize that we are not so different. It may be dark, it may hurt to admit, but we are very similar at the bottom of all this shit.

"So, how did you acquire all of your wealth?"

I anxiously ask, hoping for some knowledge of my future. The old man gives me another proud look, proud like a coach when a player makes a great play—like a teacher so proud of a student's growth.

"Well, as you might know, a troubled past makes for the best motivation. I lived my life seeing people get what I wanted, I'd seen people have what I couldn't have, and much like Warren Buffett, I fell in love with money. But not just money itself, the art of acquiring money is what fascinated me." The old man uses his left index figure and taps the left side of his temple a few times, mimicking the thinking motion.

"Money seemed like the most honest thing in the world to me, one of the only things I began to understand."

The old man lights up as he continues to talk, and the proud man I first met has arrived once again.

"From a young age, I understood being a black man puts us at an inherent disadvantage; we start behind the rest. I understood that to make it in this white man's world, we must work double--shit triple what everyone else is doing. We must have no excuses; we must claw more fierce and fight harder than anybody else. So you ask me how I acquired this wealth, well that young buck—that is a loaded question, but it all started with my drive."

The old man's look seemed to let me know that this was the answer I was looking for.

"This drive is where the "lone wolf" came from. From the moment I started working even until now, my "drive" has been my team; my ambition has been my companion, my dedication to hard work has been one of the only things I can rely on. After all of the companies, houses, women, and trips, the one thing that remains is my drive."

Again he puts his glass to the sky as if he is sharing cheers with the gods; he sips.

"Aah.."

"You see, as I've said before, I have been to many places, and at every place, I have met a woman, or in some cases, multiple women...."

The old man taps me on the left knee with his right hand as he says multiple women, insinuating his game.

"..but the women I meet see money far clearer than they see me. When you have money, you have no age; no looks, no body type; you only have dollar signs. Dollar signs seem to be the most attractive thing to girls and women of no substance."

As the words slide out, he shakes his head.

"Oh, come on…The story of you in Ibiza shows that you were having a great time with all of those "girls."

I mimic quotation marks with both hands when saying girls to mock his self-loathing. The look in my eye is calling out his bullshit because I believe that he enjoyed those moments; in all my heart, I know he did.

"I mean, you can't tell me that you don't love having the money, influence, or freedom. If I had money like you, I'd be shopping for my wife at Victoria's Secret fashion show. Ha, Ha!" I laugh out loud, proud of my joke, believing that I have proved a point.

"Ha… Yeah, go model shopping at some fashion show; sure sounds like a kid who doesn't know the true gift of life."

The old man shakes his head in disappointment, fearing that I'm not learning anything from this talk.

"What gift is that?" I ask, hinting that there is no gift greater than money and women to spend it on.

"The gift of love."

Out of all the knowledge the old man has given me this night, he seems to be vending this one-off; I begin to laugh as though his words were mockingly joked.

"Love is a gift?"

I give him a condescending head nod, not feeding into the romance of what he is saying.

"So you are going to preach to me about love? You are going to tell me what you think most about is love?"

I look at the old man as he nods his head.

"Well, isn't that the question you asked me? Didn't you want to know about my family or if I had been married?"

The old man's rhetorical retort keeps me speechless; I nod in agreement.

"I had you close your eyes earlier to visualize your girl to see exactly where your head was. I was foolish, my boy; I let work get in the way of what truly mattered. Once upon a time, I could close my eyes and see her—I could picture her walking towards me, her smell, fuck, I could even taste her. But now, at my age, I can't. At my age, the opportunity to visualize the love of my life is now lost to me. Not because of my age, or the partying, or because I have become senile, but because I chose money. But because I chose other women—because I decided to be a "lone wolf" instead of a part of the pack. I never created my pack because I was too damn foolish to see what I needed."

He sadly shakes his head.

"Well, you seem to have done not too bad as a "lone wolf," I explain, trying to cheer the old man up.

"Not too bad? I am an older man at a singles bar, talking to a knucklehead. I should be on a road trip with a family; I should be having a date night with my lovely wife; I should not be sitting here next to you."

The disappointment in the old man's voice seems paramount; it appears to be breaking him.

"Yeah, but you have the houses and the cars; you have a timepiece that people would kill for. If being a "lone wold" gets me to sit in that seat, I'd take it."

The old man nods his head, but the look on his face seems worrisome.

"Young buck, do you know what happens to a "lone wolf" when it gets old in the winter?" The old man asks with a concentrated look; onyx connects to onyx, but it feels much different this time.

I can feel the bar's movement, I know that the music is blasting, and people are talking, but for some reason, it has all gone quiet for me. I look over to the old man as words form; I shake my head confused. There must be some trick to the question, something that I haven't caught. I await the old man's answer, cautious but eager to know.

"So many people speak of being a "lone wolf" like it is commendable, like it holds some sort of valor, but there is nothing honorable about what happens to a lone wolf."

The old man pauses, only making me more anxious.

"What? What happens to the "lone wolf."

The old man views the sparkle of curiosity in my onyx; he leans in closer to me; he speaks in a whisper, but the words hold more weight than a drum.

"They starve to death, alone, and afraid with no pack around to save them."

Chapter 9: The Push

The chilling truth of the old man's statement rocks not only me, but I feel a subtle part of his life has been taken away. As our mood shifts, my body feels cold, thoughts run aimlessly, and as for the old man, it seems as if he has shaken up some things from his past.

What the old man has said is sad, it is dark, but it also appears to be the most honest thing I have ever heard. I feel sorry for the old man, but now I am also wary of my future. This sudden sadness leads me to order my fourth Sazerac, and even though his drink is almost half/empty, I better offer the old man a drink.

"Old buck, you want another Sazerac?"

I figure it is the least I can do; he's been buying me drinks all night—it wouldn't hurt to dig into my pockets for a change.

"Now, what kind of role model would I be if I had you paying for my drinks?"

The old man refuses my offer with a wave of the hand.

"Plus, I've already got our tab taken care of all night. I even picked up your first two stank ass Heinekens."

The old man laughs as he gives Braxton a head nod, then Braxton heads over to me.

"Money is no problem for me, plus I can't take it with me when I turn to dust."

The old man taps his hand on my knee, much like a grandfather would when letting one know it will be ok.

"I enjoy your company; yeah, I didn't like you so much at first, but you have grown on me."

The old man pauses for a second, looking me up and down.

"You could still use some pointers on dressing, but I'll let it slide."

Nodding with a smile on my face, laughing at the old man's jape, I begin thinking something I hadn't all night, something that would explain why this elder, billionaire, black man is at the "Rum" on this Friday. The old man says the tab is taken care of with such certainty that I must ask myself, is he the owner?

I mean, it would make sense; he is well-traveled, which would explain the decor; he has rarely had to order a drink, they always seem to be in his hand, he looks utterly unimpressed with the women or how busy the place is, and all of the workers seem on edge.

Not one of the cocktail waitresses hung around me or talked to each other, not tonight. They usually fuck around all night unless there is big money in the place or management is around. Then there was the way Braxton made each Sazerac, not rushed, but to perfection, obviously putting on a show for the owner. Even when we first met, "Are you the owner? I don't think so," the old man said that with such direction like he knew the answer. The "Rum" very well could be one of his many companies that he is just periodically coming to check on.

As Braxton descends the latter with the emerald skull, I think about how I sit with the establishment owner, getting to know him.

Do I ask for clarification? Or do I just continue with my night, enjoying the free drinks and conversation? I nervously look around the bar as though I have uncovered some rare secret that I'm having a hard time holding in.

Braxton starts the process again as I peer at him, hoping for a clue to my suspicion. He opens the bottle of absinthe, taking another whiff of the magical aroma. A good indicator of finding out if the old man is the owner will be asking Braxton if he wants a shot; nobody drinks in front of their boss, let alone their owner.

"Hey, Brax…"

I yell over the music interrupting him right before he pours the absinthe on the sugar cube that sits on the sterling silver leaf-like utensil.

"What up, Malic? You changing your drink or something?"

Braxton's voice has a slight concern as he gives me a look, worried that he had begun the process and might change my mind.

"No, nothing like that; I wanted to buy you a shot, brotha. You have been making drinks all night—I figured you might want one.

Braxton looks at me, shocked at the offer, then looks around. He then leans in on the bar like he doesn't want anyone to hear what he is about to say.

"Normally, I would, but there is ownership in tonight…."

Braxton is interrupted by a bartender before he can continue. I feel as though he was about to tell me that the man sitting next to me is, in fact, the owner he speaks of.

"Hey Brax, I need help with this Fat Tire keg on the other side."

The same bartender who brought Dee his food asks Braxton for his help.

"Damn, you girls always need something!"

Braxton teases her as he rolls his eyes at me. His Irish accent curves with every teasing word, her eyes roll simultaneously.

"Fuck you, Brax!"

She playfully punches him in the right shoulder as he laughs. Braxton pulls away from the bar.

"I'll be back, brotha; I have to go help this Ol' biddy out."

Braxton jokes as he playfully points at the bartender with his thumb. They turn and walk away, chatting about the task she needs help doing.

Although Braxton has not confirmed my thoughts, I'm now entirely sure that the old man is the owner. So, waiting for Braxton to come back and fix my drink, I figure I might pry and see if I can get the old man to come out with it.

Turning to him, feeling more clever than before, I start, "So we know why I am here, but what brings you to the "Rum" tonight?"

Man, I hope he will come out with it.

"Well, young buck, contrary to popular belief having money doesn't always award you friends, or love."

The old man states before picking up his glass for a sip.

"Oh, come on, I'm sure an attractive man like yourself, especially with all that money, you must have a few sugar babies… Shit, I know I would."

I laugh as I take a gentle swat to his left knee with my right hand. The old man takes his sip, looking at me side-eyed through the crystal glass.

"Aah."

He places the crystal glass back down on the saucer and then turns to me. We face each other as though a heated debate is about to commence, but he does not look at me just yet.

"Oh, I have had my fair share of sugar babies, gold diggers; I've had the moochers, all types of friends and women with their hands out."

The old man looks up to me.

"As you get older, you will find that all of the pseudo kindness and sexy eyes are all facades."

He states, giving a look of elder wisdom, then continues, "Young buck, you will realize one day that when all of the bottles stop coming, when the parties are over, and the dust settles, it all means shit without love and true friendship."

The old man's words pause us both; it feels like what he has said puts the entire world at a standstill.

"Money can't buy you the things that matter most. No amount of money or the places you own mean shit without people to care for, without a good woman to share them with."

The old man shakes his head, frustrated; he wishes someone would have told him the same thing at my age, and he hopes that I won't be so foolish. The angst of a lonely life exudes from the old man's pours, much more than the Sazerac ever could.

I can feel his onyx of loneliness, this hunger for love and friendship that the old man holds, as all of this angst reverberates off of him. With each word that spills from his lips, disappointment leaks out.

"After a certain point, after a certain amount of money, you get used to buying everything; sex, friendship, hell, I have even bought you tonight. I see you over there with Braxton wondering if I'm the owner or not."

The old man turns around in his chair, facing the bar. Deep-seated sadness of a less than perfect life begins leaking from each of the old man's onyx-colored eyes. Of course, alcohol has a way of getting to our deepest depressions, but the old man's grief seems unforced by the Sazerac. Instead, the accumulation of a lonely life adds fuel to his sorrow.

"You haven't bought me brotha-I—I could have left at any time, but you are the most interesting person I have ever met. You have seen more, done more, and you are way more than any of these fucks here."

I stand up next to him, putting my right hand in the middle of his back, hoping to console him. However, I'm careful not to get too close, considering we are men. Men, we're terrible about these emotions; somehow, alcohol always brings them up.

"I'm sure you haven't always felt this way; I mean, you were a lady killer back in the day."

The old man lets out a chuckle.

"Yeah, I did have a few ladies."

He says, lighting up.

"And friends, I'm sure you have had friends; I'm sure you have fallen in love; I'm sure you had all of that."

Hoping to bring up pleasant moments from his past with what I say, but words have an adverse effect. The old man's giggle turns to a grimace as he stares down into his Sazerac, but my attention to the old man is momentarily distracted as I see Braxton with my peripheral vision.

"Malic, sorry for the holdup; here is your Sazerac," Brax says as he slides my drink over to me in true bartender style. The Sazerac slides over the saucer dish and all, from where Braxton stands to my seat, without spilling a drop.

Caught trying to cheer the old man up, I missed mixing my drink, but the old man is more important than the concocting of any silly cocktail.

"Take a seat, young buck; I want to tell you something."

The old man points his hand over to my seat.

"No, actually, I think I will stand. We've been sitting most of the night."

The old man shrugs his shoulders.

"Suit yourself."

He says as I sip on my Sazerac, anxious to hear his words.

"Young buck, there is a lot that comes with having wealth, and all of that can change the person you are for better or worse. You will gain many things you have always hoped for but don't need whilst losing some of the things you need and didn't realize you wanted. Love and friendship are two of those things you might just lose if you are not careful."

The look on his face seems lonely, but the stain of guilt is most noticeable.

"You asked me before if I had ever been married or if I had kids… Then, you asked where my friends are, probably concerned with why an elderly man would be alone at this establishment on a Friday night."

I sit back down in my seat, holding my Sazerac with my left; the old man has my attention on the right.

"Well, unfortunately, some of the friends I had did pass, but two of the most important people of my life I lost way before age could ever get to them."

The old man looks to me with the onyx of pain and loss—a profound loss like death. His pain is palpable, so much so that I wish I could take it all away. I wish so dearly that I could rid the old man of the pain that torments him, of the scars he wears so deep within.

"I'm so sorry for your loss, brother."

These words flow out of my mouth and into his ears, watching as my condolence rips the wound deeper. I pat him on the back once again, trying my best to show some kind of remorse, but the old man becomes more sorrowful as this awkward tension builds.

The thoughts of the old man being the owner seem not to matter much anymore; his watch, the drinks he has bought me, it all means nothing at this point. This old man needs a friend, and I can be that friend. I am that friend.

From the tone in his voice, it sounds like he has something that he desperately needs to get off his chest. Whatever he has to say weighs on him; I can see it in his onyx and hear it in his voice. I take my seat, then pull in close to him. All I can think is to get him talking, hoping that once he speaks, it lifts the weight by releasing these words that ail him.

"How old were you when you lost these two that were so important to you?"

I ask, sincere, at full attention and genuinely caring about the answer the old man will present me.

"I was not much older than you are now, but they did not pass; they were pushed."

The old man gulps his Sazerac, a long deep drink different from anything he has done all night. I can tell this next story will hold a specific weight; the emotion he held for this next story was eerily tangible to him. The music, the bar's commotion, all of the beautiful women, nothing in the "Rum" can steal the attention away from this story.

"They were pushed?"

I ask, puzzled, fearful for a moment that he might have done something terrible in his past, but kind of sure, he wouldn't be sitting right here buying me drinks if he pushed someone to their death, let alone two people.

"Yes, I pushed them…." As the old man says it, a shocking chill runs up my back like scattered rodents in the light.

"I pushed them away."

The old man nervously rotates his crystal glass once again, looking into the liquid and seeking forgiveness. Guilt riddles his face; he takes a deep breath, the last massive gulp of his drink, and then turns back to me.

"Aah.."

He shakes his head; the sigh implies his regret, the hand on his chest proves the burn of alcohol as it descends to his stomach, and he wears the onyx of deep regret.

"You see, young buck; I was as foolish as you are. Money over love makes us all fools, I suppose, but men like you and I, well, we are the biggest fools of them all. When it comes to matters of money and matters of the heart, I seem to be as royal as a fool."

I give him a confused look as he seems to be insulting me. Here I am feeling sorry for this old man, but he continues to make japes at my expense. Leave it to this old fucker to find a way to belittle me whilst I feel compassion for him.

"I was weighing my options much like you; I was once young and ambitious just like you, and just like you, I had a woman who wanted more than I could give, or rather, more than I wanted to give. I had the wandering eye; I felt like there was always something better out there—I felt like I was better, so I began to roll out when the money started to roll in. I wanted a woman more beautiful, someone more popular; I wanted anything besides what I had right in front of me. I swear I felt like James Bond or something, feeling that love could wait, and even though I did have strong feelings for her, I ignored them."

As the old man speaks, it all feels oddly familiar. Maybe he was not trying to insult me; perhaps this is all a warning.

"My foolishness was amplified as my success began to rise. Obviously, I didn't recognize that I was a fool, but my boy warned me that my Belle..."

I put my hand up to interrupt the old man and ask, "Belle? Was that her name?" The old man shakes his head with a slight smirk.

"No, that wasn't her name, but that is what I called her most often."

The thought lights his face up, and he is happy again for a moment. The fraction of a thought he has of her brings him back to life, even if only for a split second.

"I..."

The old man looks up into the crystal chandelier hoping to see Belle's face, but I am unsure if he can.

"I-I called her Belle because she never wanted to be called princess, but to me, she was just as beautiful; scratch that, more beautiful than any Disney princess."

He gasps as he says beautiful, almost remembering something he has forgotten. The old man's tears have dissipated for the moment, but back behind his onyx, sadness still lingers.

"Devin warned me that my Belle was the woman meant for me; that before all of the money, all of the companies, all of the pseudo happiness, my Belle stood by my side. My boy warned me that the money would never grant me the satisfaction I desired; it would only amplify my flaws. With such urgency, my best friend in all the world stated that money could never buy me a family or the love needed to live a good life. My best friend, my boy, always spoke of how family starts with allowing love in and how there could never be true happiness without love and friendship, but I wouldn't listen. Devin and I started growing as businessmen, and our first business began to thrive beyond belief. As the money came, I began to change."

The intensity captured within the old man's onyx only comes from a wealth of regret. This onyx tells me that the change he endured was not necessarily the change needed for growth.

The old man seems to become more and more vulnerable as the story goes on; each word has this deteriorating effect on him. It's almost appalling how this old man sitting next to me pales compared to the larger-than-life elder statesman I first met.

"The problem with being on my own for so long is that I became used to it; I'd not needed anyone for such a long time that I began to repel love; I figured I could live without it. Living a life of poverty, a life without family, then creating a fortune of my own, changed me; it created a monster that no person was prepared to deal with."

The intense connection of onyx to onyx steals my speech; I only have magnetic ears that await the old man's words.

"I began to dive into my work, and I would do whatever was needed to further my career. Then, I began pushing my love away, thinking that money answered all problems. I failed to realize how much I loved her, how much I needed her love, and how important she was until it was too late."

The old man is almost shaking how much this story is rocking him. I can tell that to him, this was bigger than anyone passing away. This story was more than some love lost to him--he never really gave this love a chance, making this loss the most significant loss he would ever endure. As he begins to speak more, I can see Illegra every time I blink; a picture of her beautiful face stays glued to the inside of each eyelid.

"The parties came and went, the money began to pile up, and I had more women than I could count, but I had no substance in my life. My Belle was the substance needed, but I pushed her away and never let her in. Years later, I attempted to find her, I tried to get her back, but it was too late. Good women don't stay single for long, and a woman like my Belle was gone but never forgotten."

He clicks his tongue between the roof of his mouth and his teeth, tilting his head in disappointment.

"I chose the money over love. I let my truest shot at love go, and for what? Some fancy clothes, nice watches, a bunch of houses that no one sleeps in. I am most definitely the wealthiest person here, more than likely, the wealthiest person in this whole damn city; I chose the money over the love of my life, and I feel more worthless than any of these silly fucking people. I picked money over what could have been my happiest moments, over what could have been my family, my pack, but that isn't even the worst part."

The old man shakes his head with a look of self-abhorrence and bitter disdain that puts fear in me.

"What I did to my partner Devin was even more despicable than losing out on love."

He wipes his left hand down his face as though he could wipe away his past, although the old man knows he can't. The wipe of his face is that last attempt, the last hope, but not the last guilt.

"Devin was my friend, my brotha, my partner in crime. When I moved out on my own, he was the only one there for me."

I nod my head in understanding, knowing where he was coming from; it is a tough life being on your own, and sometimes friends are the only family a lonely kid has.

"When I needed food or a place to sleep, my boy was there. He was my brotha when my family wasn't around; he was better than blood to me. They say you don't go into business with friends, well that was a lie, my boy and I were great together. When we acquired the Italian company, he wrote up the proposal, and I made the in-person sale, but the logistics were all him. My boy was good with the numbers, while I was good with the words. He was a little more reserved, and I was a bit wild. After I pushed my Belle away, I became a dog. No matter the continent, the island, or even the state, I made it a point to be the biggest player around. As we began to acquire more companies, I began to acquire more women and other bad habits—I began to sacrifice our friendship. The party and popularity became blinding—this enticement of becoming a playboy billionaire seemed to be all I could chase, and the lines between what I wanted and what I needed began to blur."

At this point, the old man drops his gaze; something shameful is about to pour out of his mouth, and embarrassment flushes through every wrinkle on his face. The old man begins to rotate his right index finger around and around the rim of his empty glass. It's nervous rimming; head shakes, the connection to the glass is off. He reminds me of a child avoiding eye contact with a parent when confronted about wrongdoing.

"Devin was a family man…"

The old man begins again—his voice cracks.

"H-he was always kind and loving to his wife; h-he was a great father and an even better f-friend. Devin told me that I should have wifed up my "belle," he warned me that just because I didn't have a family growing up, that didn't mean that I couldn't have one as I grew older. He always aspired for our families to grow together; he considered me a brother, so he always saw my family as his family if I ever had one."

Tears begin to stream down the cracks of his elder-coal-umber skin.

"Maybe my jealousy got the best of me; p-perhaps it was the alcohol, or just maybe it was my a-arrogance, but at a certain point, I fucked it all up."

From his tone, the fumble of the words, and the sorrow that leaks from the onyx, I can tell where this was going; I know what comes next.

"You know what leaves and never comes back?"

The old man asks rhetorically. I shake my head, hoping not to take anything more away from him. He looks back up; onyx connects to leaking onyx; he can sense my compassion—I can read the old man feels he's unworthy of sympathy. I can read within his onyx that more than sorrow lingers, more than contempt and regret; within the onyx of his eyes read something that I might not be prepared to interpret.

"Yesterday… When yesterday is gone, it's gone, and you could never get it back. I could never get my Belle back; I slept with Devin's wife, and I could never take that back."

My gut fills with this nervous knot, almost as though I had committed the crime, feeling the old man's embarrassment almost as if it were mine to bear.

"I ruined a lifelong friendship with the only man that was family to me, with a man I built companies with, with a man I built memories with; with a man that I loved more than a brother. I threw it all away because of my arrogance and my lunacy."

I want to ask the old man how he could do such a thing. I want to know how low he had gotten to hit the sheets with his best friend's wife. I could never see myself doing that to one of the "boys," never; never, and I want to know how he could ever do such a thing.

Witnessing the old man's onyx of embarrassment, I wish I had advice I could give the man; I wish I could be here for him in some way more than shaking my head with this befuddled expression. I'm amazed that a man who seems so great could be so broken. I'm surprised that a man so wealthy could be so alone. I am in utter shock that a man that seemed so put together is, in fact, broken.

I have always heard that money can't buy happiness, but never have I seen it. I can't believe that this man I was spending the night idolizing; he has been where I want to go, he has seen what I want to see, he has gotten the thing that I want to get, but he just might be the most insecure and unhappy person I have ever met. I have no words to say, and my thoughts are now clouded with the old man's regret.

"As you get older, the looks fade, the "cool" stuff becomes placid, and the parties are all so dull. You will learn in life; all of the world's money can't change the fact that the most essential parts of existence are priceless; truly priceless."

He looks down into his empty glass, shaking his head in regret, as a teardrop sneaks into his glass as he dwells on the past. I solemnly nod my head in agreement, politely trying to ignore the old man as he fights back tears. I'm speechless; nothing can be said, no words for the moment or witty observation.

I have spent most of my life with the ability to lighten up the mood, often offering a shot when a friend is sad or commenting on some clever remark to get people's minds off the most challenging parts of life, but this time, I have nothing. The old man sits, rotating his glass round and round, almost trying to hypnotize himself, working so hard to forget.

"I'm sorry that all of that happened to you. I'm sorry that you have ended up here, but you have me now, buddy. I'll be here for you. I am your friend."

The sincerity in my voice is well received at first, but then a reaction happens. The old man festers on what I've said for a moment, but as he nods his head, I can feel his frustration grow.

"You don't understand, young buck; you're not listening. I don't need another friend; I don't need some new woman to romance, and I don't need your fucking sympathy."

The old man's churlish retort shoves me back to the beginning of the night, and his tears stop.

"My friend?... You don't even know my name, what I do, or where I live."

He turns to look at me, taking his eyes off his empty glass.

"No, after tonight, we will never see each other again; you will forget this night ever happened, and I will go back into hiding as I did before this night. You will likely wake up tomorrow with little to no hangover as you go on with your young life—forgetting about the old man and his pitiful Sazerac."

The old man looks back into his empty crystal glass, contemplating everything I don't know. He is shaking his head ever so slightly, thinking that everything we have spoken of is all for not. But then the old man looks back to me with a different sparkle in his onyx; there is a softness in them, this look of revitalized patience.

The old man balls his hand in a fist, then coughs into it. It is not so much a cough as it clears his throat. He clears his throat of the cracks, sorrow, and flem developed by the thick liquor; he clears his throat to cough up some of the rage created by my foolishness. The old man looks are me with the onyx of optimism, then begins again.

"I tell you all of this not to gain your sympathy but to impart some wisdom onto you."

Intently onyx connects to onyx, almost piercing my soul down to the core; he leans closer to me.

"When I was younger, I had no one to tell me of such things; I had no person who had experienced life as I had or had known a person that went through the same trials. When I was younger, I had never seen a wealthy black man; hell, I had never had a positive black male role model my entire life. I had to look toward NBA players and actors who could care less about a young black man that was alone in the world. I tell you all of these things in hopes that you will not make the same mistakes that I had; in hopes that you will become a better person than I am."

The old man's eyes water again, but I am unsure why. By this moment, I can't tell if the old man is drunk or is just really trying to prove a point, but still, I listen.

"Why are you here, Malic?"

The old man asks, using my name for the first time all night. It never occurred that the old man might know my name or even cared, but here he is saying it.

"I…I don't know the drinks, I suppose, the women. May-maybe the atmosphere."

I shudder, confused as to why he would ask me that question; isn't it obvious being at the bar why I'm here?

"But why have you chosen to sit with me all night?"

The old man asks without searching for an answer; I shake my head and curl my lips, unsure of my retort. I'm a little fearful that this might be another one of his elder japes at my youth's expense, and I am not ready for another jab about the person I am; I wait for the old man's response to my silence.

"You see, the sad thing, young buck, is I was you many years ago; I was in the same seat as you. I was a fool…"

The old man looks down at his watch before continuing.

"Much like you, I wanted the shiny things, I wanted the women, and I knew I needed the money to get those things. I sacrificed so much to eventually end up right here, next to you, sitting in "your seat.""

His reference to the beginning of the night lets me know that he might not be intoxicated; he is just as coherent as when we first met. His subtle reference to the beginning of the night also reminds me of how far this conversation has progressed.

"You believe that everything costs, don't you? You probably have the notion that money will solve everything, right?"

I nod; the old man shakes him, disappointed by my foolishness.

"You've probably spent a good deal of your life figuring out how to acquire the money to get those things you want and build the life you think you want. You more than likely spend moments by yourself thinking of what it will all cost."

The old man skips a beat for a second while I quietly nod, then he continues.

"And you would be right; everything in life does have a price, and believe it or not, every woman costs something. Whether it is the escort you buy for the night, the pretty sugar babies you buy things for, or even the woman of your dreams, there will always be a cost. Anything worth having has a cost, young buck; everything in life has some price to pay, even the woman of your dreams. But what a dream woman costs, most young men like yourself aren't willing to pay, and by the time you realize that price, it will be too late."

Puzzled by the old man's pithy statement, I sit quietly in thought. After all of his talk about money and how it can't buy everything, he states that my dream woman will cost something, that everything worth having has a cost?

Once again, this old man is playing me for a fool—once again, this old man is toying with my emotions, twisting my mind in knots with confusing metaphors and pessimistic views of life, love, and friendship. He knows not of the person I am; he only assumes.

The old man expects that I will go down his reckless path and make the witless decisions he has, but he and I have nothing in common. His mistakes will not be mine. I will not end up alone, with a Sazerac, at some silly bar, and I would never embarrass or shame myself in the ways that he has.

"What does a dream woman cost? What price will I have to pay?"

I ask snarky, sure that he is only trying to yank my chain by confusing me further.

"She will cost the price of your heart."

The old man's accent sounds profound as he takes his right index finger, leans over to me, then points it into the middle of my chest. After, he leans back in his chair and continues.

"She will cost your heart, young buck, your sacrifice, and your time; she will cost much more than all the jewels in the sea. She is the cost of the easiest thing you had to give her, which is your love. That's what love is, it's sacrifice, it's time, it's friendship, it's advice, it's understanding, it's listening, and it is so much more than money. Love is sticking around for an argument because you will get through it and get through it together. Love is all the good that comes after the bad; it is that warm connection of onyx to sapphire. As you get older, your time with friends will fade, your work will fade, your looks will fade, and when all of these things disappear, you will have wished that you had paid that price to keep her. When you become my age, you will have wished you gave her your time; you will have wished that you sacrificed for her. Then, when you are an elderly man sitting alone at a bar, you will realize something; you will realize that the one price that you should have paid was the easiest price to pay, and for that price, you would have received a prize that no amount of money in the world could ever buy you. No amount of companies or trinkets could amount to the greatest prize you would have gotten. Love would have been that prize, and you would have cherished that prize more than any watch or home or any trip that all of your money would have brought you."

Chapter 10: Number Five

As would elephants on eggshells, the old man's words have begun to crack

me. He seems to be talking directly to my soul, each syllable targeting my

foolishness, each consonant carefully constructed to combat my cowardly lack

of coherence. The old man speaks as though he were sitting in the room, right there, as I broke Illegra's heart. The combination of sharp looks and profound words that spill from elder lips leaves this eerie feeling that holds me, almost sobers me. I grab my Sazerac off the saucer dish, hoping to wash down some realism, but the old man starts again. He must see that his words affect me; he must feel there is more to say.

"Young buck, at some point in your life, you will have to decide what is more important to you."

Raising from his seat for the first time all night, the old man walks over to me. It is a short step from stool to stool, but he must feel my youth threatening to take over. I try running from the conversation, using my Sazerac as a scapegoat, but the old man steps in closer to me. He places his left hand on my upper back, then takes his right index finger and begins tapping my chest, right where the heartbeats. He forcefully taps my chest multiple times, disrupting my ability to drink, almost hurting me with each poke.

The smell of past Sazeracs and lavender cologne fill the air; this is the closest we have been all night. Looking at his onyx, I can see his years' wrinkle, threatening to confess his age. His hands shake ever so slightly; he's having difficulty lifting them. This old man seems to be aging as the night progresses, as if each story told adds years of depression. I put my glass down on the bar, giving him my attention.

"Young buck, you will have to decide what is important here…."

The old man looks deep into the coal of my onyx but speaks of my heart.

"You will have to decide what truly makes your heart beat. Is it the money, the trinkets, the women?"

The old man pauses, putting his palms to the ceiling, displaying the "Rum" as though it is my prize to have.

"The bars, the nightclubs, or will you be smarter than all of that?"

The old man squints, searching within my onyx for answers he knows I do not have.

"Will you do as I did, putting the money before the love, the sex before the women? Or will you grow better than I did?"

The old man's voice seems to be cracking more and more, and as he turns to hobble back to his stool, I'm given cause to pause.

My drink is half warm, about half empty, but this conversation has made me feel half full of shit. Here I was going through life working to become wealthy, believing that wealth was the path to happiness, but next to me sits a man as rich, if not more affluent, than I could ever hope to be. Next to me sits a man who speaks of love and not money. Right next to me, in the very next seat, this old man says he would have picked the love of his life over all of the money in the world

I look at the old man as he gets back in his seat; his movement is slow, making apparent why he hasn't gotten up before. I suppose this rise from his seat means to prove a point, yet, I don't see why he would go through all the effort?

"Are you telling me that if you could take it all back, you'd choose love over money if you could turn back time? Overall of your success? Over everything you have built in the last, however many years?"

My query means to remind the old man of what he has built, of all that he has accomplished. I need to know if he feels that all of his accolades meant nothing. I must know what it's "all" worth.

"One-hundred percent."

The old man's response happens without a second thought, and as onyx connects to onyx, all I feel is his honesty.

"Young buck, what is success with no people to share in your glory? What is a house without love—without a family to make it home?"

I have no answer for his questions, no witty retort to help with the loss of his "phantom family."

It is said that when a limb has been cut off, the disabled can still have feeling around that area; it is said that there is specific energy that remains after the arm or leg has gone. They call it a "phantom limb," and much like a "phantom limb," within the onyx of the old man's eyes lives the absence; lives his phantom family.

I finish my half-full Sazerac in two quick gulps, frightened by the old man's eyes. He sits, visualizing a past that could have been but never will, at a momentary loss for words. The old man looks within the empty glass, searching for a life he can never have, becoming morose with every gleam, envious of the light. It is astonishing how all of the wealthy arrogance has disappeared; he doesn't seem as sharp, as smooth, and this elder person next to me is but a shade of the man I admired at first glance.

Our conversation and the feels have been so deep that I had not realized how late it had become. As I look around the bar, it is not as packed as it once was, and employees are doing what is needed to finish their shift. There are still a few people here; drunken voices can be heard on the other side of the bar; newfound hookups blossom in the moonlight, but the rush that once was is no more.

This ambiance of a Friday night coming to a close is all around. Music plays but is not blaring, people are giving final farewells, the ring of bartenders closing out tabs echo in the background, and there are still a few cute women here, but my only concern is the well-being of the old man.

His demeanor is so distraught. The glow of a confident billionaire has completely dissipated, and in the few hours of our conversation, he has let go of his supercilious nature, the superiority he once had. No, now he honestly seems like an old man alone, with just his Sazerac, and with every rotation of the glass, he appears to be fading away.

I wonder what he sees when he looks into the glass? What looks back at him? I wonder what memories materialize in the crystal reflection?

A major downfall of mine is that I am no good with grief or even consoling; I don't understand the sentiment. I've been on my own for too long, so remorse is not one of my more exceptional traits. If ever I've been down and out, I have ways of running away, an exit strategy. I'll come to a bar, hit the gym, or pull myself out of the rut on my damn own somehow, someway. I'm not good with emotions, "Leggy" often has comments about my lack of empathy.

Illegra has always wanted me to be more open and honest about how I genuinely feel, but I can't. She believes it would make me more caring toward others and more understanding if I confronted my demons, but I won't.

Frankly, the entire conversation makes me feel uncomfortable, which causes me to leave the room or turn on some Netflix or something—anything to get me out of my head. So used to steering clear of emotions, I typically run, but this time around, at this very moment, I feel for the old man.

I may not know his name, hell, I've only known the man for a few hours, but I find myself concerned for his well-being for reasons unknown to me.

But before diving in on these emotions, the buzzed part of my mind wants another Sazerac; that or my youth is putting up one final fight. So I throw one hand up to grab Braxton's attention. He seems busy cleaning up a well on the far end of the bar, just a bit away from me. I wave my left hand from side to side, hoping to grab his attention, but he keeps cleaning.

Braxton looks up, glances at me, and then looks back down into the well; he is shaking his head in irritation, muttering words to himself. He continues washing the bar-well, blatantly ignoring me. I get out of my seat—look back at the old man, put one finger up, "Give me a sec, old buck," then walk to the bar's end, where Braxton is elbow deep into the well.

"Brax, brotha, can I get one last Sazerac before the night ends completely."

Braxton gives me a puzzled look, pulls away from his cleaning, then starts.

"Hey, bud, are you sure you want another drink? You don't want some water or some pretzels or something?"

He leans in on the bar giving me a concerned look, hinting that he believes I have had maybe my fill of Sazeracs. I look over to my right back by my seat, looking at the old man's depressed state, then turn back to Braxton.

"Yeah, I'm sure; I've got to cheer him up, and the Sazerac will cheer me up in the process."

I laugh while Braxton gives me another puzzled, unsure look. He squints his eyes, sizing me up, staring into me with the emerald of concern. He seems to be weighing in on my intoxication, wondering if another Sazerac is what I need.

"Plus, Brax, I've only had four of these Sazeracs, and you've seen me way more fucked up than this."

Hopefully, my wink pairs well with my drunken—drinking logic; Braxton looks back, arching his bottom lip, scratching his chin as though this motion will help with his decision.

"Ok, Malic, I'll make you one last Sazerac, but I'm closing shop after this."

Braxton gives me a reluctant nod of approval before walking away to gather all he needs to make the final Sazerac of the night. I don't get why Braxton is acting so weird with me; guaranteed, I have been way more inebriated than I am right now, but fuck him let me check on the old man.

While Braxton grabs everything needed for one last Sazerac, I hop in my seat, then turn it around, facing the old man.

"Getting another drink, I see?"

The old man sounds as disappointed as a proud father, slightly smirking up at me. I nod my head.

"Yeah, I need another Sazerac to cheer your old ass up."

I look down at the old man's left hand to see a new glass filled with that brownish-pink liquid. Somehow this old fucker already has a drink.

"I beat you to the punch, young buck. Trying to "learn you" got me so depressed I needed another. It has been a while since my last one."

The old man chuckles, tilting his drink in my direction.

"How did you get a drink so fucking fast?"

He has got to be the owner or a partner or something; mutha fucka has had a drink in his hand all night.

"An old man has tricks, young buck; an old man has tricks."

The old man looks at Trixie at her end of the bar, gives her a wink, blows her a kiss, then takes a sip.

"Aah."

It all makes sense now. Trixie has been hooking his old ass up; no wonder Braxton has been grabbing all of the tools needed from the other side of the bar, which he happens to be doing at this very moment.

"Is that number five for you?"

The old man points in Braxton's direction, who seems to be making this Sazerac faster than before; that or my attention might not be what it once was.

"Yeah, it's number five...."

I tilt my head and curl my bottom lip in disbelief as the old man does the same. I turn, facing the bar, glancing at Braxton as he begins to pour that "magical elixir" over the sterling silver leaf-like utensil that holds a sugar cube. My eyes fixate on the liquid as it shrinks the cube with each drop. The liquid in the miniature wine glass begins to cloud, and as Braxton sets the fountain to drip, the enchantment of the concoction catches me yet again.

Braxton grabs the bottle of Woodford, pours it into his mixing glass, pours the cognac, three dashes of Peychaud's, three bits of angostura, fills the stirring glass with ice, then stirs. Every time the silver spoon hits the glass's inside, the rhythmic stirring echoes in my ear. Cling-Cling! It echoes louder. Cling! The stirring of ice and liquid. Cling-Cling! The stirring, the sound of metal to glass, all sound so harmonious. Cling-Cling! Cling!

Next, Braxton grabs the crystal rock glass and pours the Absinthe within it for the final time I observe. Braxton swirls the glass around and around, coating every part inside the glass with the "magical elixir." He makes sure that every piece inside the crystal rocks glass has a thick layer of Absinthe. As he contorts his wrist back and forth, I witness Braxton's love for his craft even down to the last Sazerac. He carefully observes the glass and then places it on the saucer dish. Then, Braxton puts the strainer on top of his mixing glass after removing his silver mixing spoon; he then pours the brownish-pink finished product into the crystal rock glass. Finally, for the last time, Braxton cuts a perfect rectangle of lemon peel that he places on the saucer, accompanying the finished and final Sazerac.

"And there you go, Malic, your final Sazerac of the night," Braxton says, less frustrated than when he began.

Braxton carefully emphasizes the end of my drinking with a cold stare. Emerald connects to onyx, hoping that I get the message. I give Braxton a head nod before grabbing the lemon peel. I express it over the drink, allowing lemon zest to make its way into my Sazerac. I then rub the lemon peel around the entire rim of the crystal rocks glass to ensure my lips get every taste of lemon as soon as the glass touches. Finally, I drop the skin within the glass, allowing it to sink, becoming engulfed within the magical drink. As the lemon skin floats back up to the top of the glass, I turn to the old man, giving him one of our final cheers; but before we sip, I lift my glass to the crafty hands that made it, Braxton.

Braxton gives me a nod as a thank you, then walks over to his sink and pours a glass of water. After pouring the glass of water, Braxton walks with it back over to me; emerald connects to onyx, then he places the glass of water right next to the saucer where my Sazerac will sit. Braxton slides the water right in my line of sight. I look at the glass of water, then onyx connects to emerald, and emerald connects back to the intoxication of onyx. I shrug off Braxton's look and bring the Sazerac to my mouth, taking a long sweet sip.

My lips feel a refreshing burst of lemon zest from top to bottom as they connect with the glass. As I tilt the crystal rocks glass, the chilling liquid slides down my tongue, electrifying every taste bud, each one dancing in delight. There is a virtual party in my mouth as this drink varnishes my throat, and the aroma only heightens the taste.

The Absinthe clears my sinuses; the mixture of bitters, rye whiskey, and cognac plays at my imagination, and for the last time, I feel blessed with the most excellent cocktail ever created. My eyes close, my lips smack, and my throat tingles.

"Aah.."

Chapter 11: Futurum Se

"So where will the night take you after this? Where do you call home?"

I ask the old man before taking another sip of my Sazerac.

"Aah."

More than likely, this will be the last drink we have together, so I try lightening the mood with casual conversation. The old man holds the crystal rocks glass to his lips for a spell, then takes a sip without saying a word.

"Aah."

Everyone has left. Chris and his crew of numbskulls are gone, the rift-raft of youngsters has cleared out, and all the beautiful women have found their way home or wherever the night will lead them. So now it is me, the old man, and our Sazeracs; well, and Braxton, of course.

Heavy lingers this eerie feeling as my questions hang out in the open. I'm not sure how the old man will react, but it is about the only thing I could manage to ask.

"Don't worry about what I'm doing after this; stay focused, young buck. What are YOU going to do?"

The old man holds his Sazerac in his right hand while pointing directly to my heart with his left index finger.

"I'm sure that your "friend" Chris has the idea of checking on Illegra, "SEEING" if she's doing all right."

He takes a lite bite of his bottom lip, gives me a head nod, then turns back to face the bar.

The old man mocks quotations hinting that Chris might use this night as the perfect reason to contact Illegra, taunting me with the word "seeing" because of remarks I made earlier in the night. I sip my drink, then place the Sazerac back down on the saucer whilst facing the bar. I look into the enchanted liquor shelf, then begin rotating the crystal rocks glass on the dish.

Peering down into the elixir as it twirls, I hope some form of an answer will float up. So I look, and I look at the liquor funnels; as the Sazerac spins, hoping to make sense of it all—I hope that anything can make sense of my doltish impulse.

There is a bright note within the rind written in black letters with the phrase, "GO HOME," for only my eyes to see. Is the Sazerac toying with my mind? Maybe this old man is right? Chris, seeing me here, my fight with Illegra; it all might be the perfect ammo for that flash fucker to make his move.

My chest begins rising in a fury, my breath is deep, my lips twitch, and then I take an apprehensive sip of my Sazerac as the old man's words dig deep. Never have I been nervous about losing Illegra, and I have never felt threatened by that dullard Chris, but right now, that grasp that once I had seems to falter. I shake my head as if I disagree with the old man, attempting to shed my fear that his assessment might very well be correct.

Illegra is such a great woman, but I have treated her less. She has been there for me as I grow, giving me a place to stay, let me drive her car and things—anything to make me feel welcomed. Illegra encourages me, supports me, and is always right there for me, but what do I give her in return?

I can feel the old man peering at me as I rethink the man I have been for Illegra or lack thereof, then his words start yet again.

"Young buck, I keep trying to tell you that we," the old man uses his left thumb pointing at himself and then points to me, "are not so different."

The old man takes a sip, places the Sazerac on the saucer, then turns to face me. He seems to be gearing up for yet another story, having more knowledge to impart, but I'm tired of his words. And I find myself flummoxed by the nature of his stories, his insight; it is all affecting me that I'm not prepared for.

Currently, my face is wrinkled with exhaustion and slight defeat; I feel beat up by this night. Here I intended to cheer the old man up or at least lighten the mood; instead, he states plans for my defeat, and at the hands of Chris no less. Every time I try changing the subject or ask common questions, the old man finds a way to bring up love and complications. I find myself frustrated by his words, beset by the old man's life, but I know he speaks the truth deep down.

The old man SMACKS! Me on the right shoulder with the back of his right hand, slowing the twirl of my glass—hoping to bring me back to reality. I've been rotating the glass so intently that I have turned the Sazerac into a woebegone cyclone that I wish would suck this feeling away. The old man begins talking before I can look up, but he knows I listen.

"You see, I didn't tell you what exactly happened to me and my love; with my Belle. I not only pushed her away, but I lost her—I lost her to a man, much like Chris."

I look to my right, lifting my gaze to the old man as he leans in. He clasps his fingers together, leaning in deep, close to me. If our conversation on this night were a big glorious cake, I'm sure this next story would be the icing. I stop fidgeting with my half-full Sazerac to look at the old man, viewing the onyx of true compunction.

What more could have happened to the old man to make him so lonely, so regretful? Even though I feel a bit sorry about my situation with Illegra, I must know what happened to the old man. What happened to create this person who sits next to me? I look to the old man, giving him the same attention he has deserved all night. Onyx connects to onyx.

"In everyone's life, there is a turning point--the point where everything changes, and you change. Sometimes you know it right away, sometimes you don't realize it until much later, but you will know… I always knew I loved my Belle; I knew I didn't want to lose her, but I had an ass-backward way of showing it. I believed I was doing everything needed to keep her, but I was sadly mistaken. Rather, I used the excuse that my success—that my money would be what we needed to build a family…"

The old man looks down at his lap, shaking his head. As I gaze at the old man, I try not to make it evident that this is so familiar to me; I am relating in such an intense way that it frightens me. So instead of speaking, I can only nod my head—eyes peeled like a wordless dullard.

"I would network nightly, spending nights out of bed answering emails, taking long phone calls, canceling date nights, all in the name of growing wealth. I used the ruse that building my success was for our future, that everything I did was for her. I-I neglected the woman I loved to chase money."

The old man hangs his head as his voice cracks. His lips are dry, wrinkled, and trembling. His cheekbones drop as though his skin might slide completely off, and he shakes as though every year of heartache lives within this last story.

"I-I always knew I-I loved her, but around my friends, I acted as if I didn't r-remember or didn't care."

The old man unclasps his hands and then balls up his left into a fist. He coughs into his hand, clearing his throat. This cough is not calm and polite like earlier in the night; no, this is the type that sounds of clogged mucus, regret, desolation; a real hacking cough that echos throughout the bar, and then the old man continues.

"When my boy Devin explained that my Belle was my woman, he saw that she needed to be my wife; he knew that she was the only person that could truly make me happy. Then, years later, when my Belle was not my wife, I used that anger as an excuse to ruin Devin's marriage. The pain I caused myself, losing my Belle then losing Devin, became my anger, making my resentment as much a part of me as my wealth."

As the old man leans back into his stool, I sip in what he says. He is looking past me into the distance, and letting these words out seems to give him this disturbing calm. The old man remains quiet, yet the onyx screams of regret, disappointment, and loneliness all within the clouds of onyx. He stays silent for a moment, then shakes it off. The onyx begins to gloss, then his voice breaks.

"I...I was too damn prideful to admit I loved my Belle; t—to admit I did it all for her...."

A stream of sadness leaks from the onyx down the old man's wrinkled cheekbones, climbing over each wrinkle and those new wrinkles that seem to come from nowhere.

"I was too damn prideful to admit that she was the love of my life and that I needed her. Every day, even after she moved on, married, had kids, even grandkids, she was the one treasure I still wanted; even after she passed, my Belle was the one prize that my money could never buy."

The old man wipes the tears off his face with his left hand as his head shakes in bitter turmoil and absolute disappointment. His movement is not smooth or put together; this man is broken.

"So you see, young buck, I have walked in your shoes, I have sat in that seat, and if you give men like Chris a chance, you will lose her. If you keep neglecting what you are, then that which once was yours will soon be another man's.

"My Belle married another man; they had kids; they lived a happy life. Sure, I have the money; I have been to all of the places, and I have slept with all of the women, but true happiness was another man's and not my own."

The old man turns around, grabs his Sazerac, then takes a solemn sip.

"Aah."

Shocked with not much to say, I sit stewing as I begin to soak up exactly what it all means.

"Man, that's heavy."

My feeble words receive silence as we both hang our heads.

Is this going to be me at some point? Am I going to look back on my youth regretful, filled to the brim with remorse? Will I be lonely with no friends, no family, just my thoughts of the past, reflecting on things too late to fix? What about Illegra? What if, at this very moment, Chris or some other fellow is reaching out to her, promising her the world, giving even more reason for her to find someone better? Maybe wealth isn't everything? Perhaps this old man is right?

It has been said that money can't buy happiness, which I've jokingly remarked, 'Only broke folks say that shit,' but now I've seen it up close. Now I am shocked by the truth in what I thought to be a silly-ass statement.

I nervously glance over to the old man who is penitently looking in his glass. We are like two peas in a shitty ass pod, sitting here, looking into liquor for answers. The old man's regret has shown me a glimpse into my future if I continue down this path—if I continue to deny what I've always known.

Thinking of the night, of the old man's words, of Illegra, something comes over me. There is something profound inside of me that relates to this man; the loneliness of my future, my mother's drug problem, the absentee father, the suicide of my sister, the family that disowned me; like a ton of bricks, the emotion of what loneliness looks like lands on me. Then, like a Sunday linebacker, all of the darkness of my past rushes into me; I become choked up.

I try to catch myself mentally, but I am not good with emotions. Something is happening to me; I feel at a loss for breath, but I can breathe—my mouth is becoming dry as the onyx slowly starts to water—my heart is beating sporadically. It feels like I will cry, and the last thing I need is Braxton or the old man seeing tears in my eyes. Braxton already thinks I am drunk, but so will the old man if I begin to cry right here.

Hopefully, this deep swallow of saliva will alleviate some emotional pressure. I swallow, but to no avail; my anguish only grows. Ultimately, after the weight becomes too much to bear, I get up out of my seat, put one finger up to let the old man know, 'give me a second,' then say, "I'll be back, brotha; I'm going to the bathroom." I make sure to throw bass in my voice to cover the broken oration. I avoid the connection of onyx, as I am sure the old man will recognize my grief. He gives a slight nod but says nothing. As I walk away towards the bathroom, leaving my Sazerac on the bar half-full, I look back at the old man and stop.

The old man looks to me with the onyx of contrition; onyx stays connected to onyx as I stand in the middle of an empty bar—surrounded by vacant seats. Then something between the old man and I connects for just a moment, even from where I stand. He holds his left hand up in the air giving support from a distance. Oddly enough, this feels similar to a goodbye.

The "Rum" is empty, the lights are brighter, and Braxton is the only bartender left. The cocktail waitresses are gone, the cleaning crew has just arrived, then the music stops, almost precisely on cue with my emotions.

The old man puts his hand down, gives me a head nod, and then faces the bar, grabs his Kangol hat off the bar, and puts it on. He turns the brim to the front like a former golfer or something, preparing for an exit. Then he grabs his Sazerac and takes a sip. Looking at the old man, it's as though I have jumped forward in time to glimpse at my future.

Alone, at the bar with his Sazerac and only the resentments of the past to keep him company, the old man sits. The bartender says no words to the man; he has no friends, no woman, and no phone calls that await his answer. So he just sits at the bar, the old man and the Sazerac, alone in the world.

It saddens me to see such a sight; the light is bright, but the darkness of the old man's loneliness is horrifying, like a cloud of gloom. I'm not one to scare easily, fear is for suckas, but tonight I've come face to face with it. Tonight I know fear, and it is making me sick.

Is this my future? Is the old man the person I am meant to become? And is my destiny full of nights alone staring at my past through a crystal rocks glass, through a Sazerac?

I look back at the old man one last time as I ascend out of the dome-like seating, unsure of the answers I seek. As my eyes begin to water, I turn from my gaze at the old man and then head to the bathroom. Tears run down my face uncontrollably as I approach the mahogany door. I try breathing, hoping that the sigh will alleviate the sorrow, but I am not so lucky. My tears burn like acid, wreaking havoc and corroding me from the outside.

I open the mahogany door, enter the bathroom, and instantly begin balling. Recalcitrant tears like never before begin racing down my face; I feel like life has been taken from me. Alcohol and Absinthe all catch up to me as though Mike Tyson has administered a knockout punch. Intoxicated sorrow overtakes me as all four and a half of the Sazerac rip through every emotion I have ever had. I feel like I'm looking through a glass of pitiful water—drowning in my doltish resolve.

The pain that fills my eyes is a liquid that comes out clear and thick; dense tears of penitence and unrest. The room starts to spin; my equilibrium is off-kilter. A pounding develops in my head; it feels like a stampede, bass that rumbles and vibrates my whole body. Then my stomach begins to turn with disappointment, much as it would turn from sickness. I start sweating and overheating; my body temperature rises. I stumble over my feet; gas moves from my rumbling belly escaping out of my mouth, and then,

"Bwaaaap!"

This funk that floats up into my nostrils turns my stomach; it turns in such a way that I run to one of the bathroom stalls. Dinner and liquor rush out of my belly, finding a home within the toilet bowl. Big chucks fall hard and loud; small pieces fly in all directions, even some parts outside and on the toilet seat. I stumble back out of the stall, wiping my face, appalled at what I have become.

Where am I? Who am I at this moment? Is this the man I want to become, this drunken dullard stumbling around and in a bar bathroom, puking his brains out?

When I looked at the old man, my life flashed before the onyx as though it were a brace with death—this fear unlike anything I have ever felt before. I begin walking over to one of the bathroom sinks, thinking of what this all means.

I grab the sink with both hands, looking up into the mahogany framed mirror. The crimson onyx blurs my vision as the intoxication of a reality that might be my future repeatedly drips from each eye.

"Is that me out there?!"

I yell at myself, pointing my fingers, signaling what awaits me outside the door.

"Is that the fucking person you want to be?!"

I angrily scream at myself, echoing throughout the whole bathroom.

"What the fuck is wrong with you?"

I yell once again as though the man staring back can answer. Repeatedly I shake my head, looking down as each teardrop plunges into the porcelain sink. My eyes begin to swell, and my nose starts to drip as the reality of what I could become sits outside waiting for me. I grab a paper towel to blow the snot and regret out of my nose, then throw it away.

Frantically, almost shamefully, like a foolish adolescent, I use the back of both my hands to wipe the liquid idiocy from my eyes. I turn on the water faucet, both cold and hot, gather water in the palms of my hands, then attempt to wash the resentment, the shame, and the doltish impulse off of my face. I look into the mirror, onyx connects to an egregious reflection of onyx, and I am appalled by the man looking back. His eyes are glossy, but the coal's focus shows a truth he has never noticed before. Within the onyx, I see a future that he wanted to forget, but I want to remember—I must remember.

"Illegra is a great woman; she needs a great man."

I speak to myself like a lesson of precisely what I need to hear. Then, I grab the sink from both ends, pulling myself close to the mirror again. I pull my face so close that I am almost kissing glass with my nose; the Eskimo Kiss of intoxication. This motion is the only war to take a more in-depth look into the onyx of a coward; I want to understand why I've acted so doltishly.

"What are you afraid of? Why are you so convinced that you don't deserve happiness? Or Love?"

My life has always been dark, full of absent thoughts, so why would I push the opportunity away when love presents itself? Illegra is a great woman, she deserves a great man, and we both deserve happiness. I pause for a moment, looking away from the mirror, down into the sink. Then, letting the word soak in, I stand sniffling. There is this warming feeling from the top of my head down to my vibrating toes as the night cycles through my mind.

I will be that man; I am that man; it might have just taken this night to realize it, but I am the man for Illegra. Maybe the fifth Sazerac is a realization of what we run from—perhaps this entire night is to make me see what I was scared to admit? I look up into the mirror, deep into the onyx one last time. The faucet still runs, water hits the porcelain echoing throughout the bathroom, and I'm stuck as my thoughts reverberate throughout my entire doltish body and mind.

I have been drunk many times and in this bathroom, but tonight is different. This magical elixir has taken hold of me; it has grabbed my thoughts and emotions and taken control of my being. This night, the elixir and the old man showed me what I could not see before. Turning off the faucet, I then close my eyes and visualize.

First, I see the heart shape of her puckered lips and the sharpness of her chin. This vision is dark, she is in shadows, but her skin glows, almost angelic—like a light at the end of my dark tunnel. Her alabaster skin warms as the sapphire magically entraps me, pulling me in, this blue, a blue more vibrant than the sky; seductively intoxicating—more potent than any drug.

Next, her beautiful long black hair, like a velvet sheet, shining crisp and bright. Even in darkness, her hair shines, this celestial glow, the actual envy of the gods. The beauty that is Illegra is even more apparent than before, and the darkness behind her is the fear that I was not good enough—the doubt that I might not be worthy, but she shines brighter than that fear; now, there is no reason for doubt. I love Illegra, something that I have always known but often denied.

With each tear that slides down my cheekbones, I feel parts of who I was and who I might be washing away. Yet, as I view each drop descend into the porcelain sink, I realize it all means.

I look up into the mirror for the final time, onyx connects to onyx, and for the first time, in many months, maybe even years, I recognize the onyx looking back.

Chapter 12: The Old Man

Washing my hands, my face, washing off this feeling, I work to bring

myself back to reality. The water runs warm, and my heart slows its beat, but

these thoughts still simmer. I can not be sure if it is the Sazerac or if my

emotions toy with me, but this feeling is foreign, as my reactions are inconsistent. I'm feeling weak and vulnerable; I feel like change is happening. I take a deep breath.

Looking into the onyx one last time, I wonder if this whimpering fool will disappear? Sure hope so; who knows how long I have been sulking in here? Or what awaits me outside?

Calmly I wash my face, then dry my hands. In a way, it feels like I'm wiping away some of the foolishness, cleaning off the dirt of my doltish actions. As though I am shaking away all of the fear I have come accustomed to, this uncertainty. The dispenser echos, bouncing off the black tile as I pull down a couple of paper towels; I feel off-balanced yet better than before. Drying these trembling hands helps clear this moist feeling of doubt and helps do away with these latent drops of uncertainty. I am preparing myself for a new belief, giving myself some much-needed courage as I get ready to finish this night and face the old man.

I turn off the faucet, then SMACK! The collision of each hand to each cheek stings but well worth the wake. I then walk up to the mahogany door; inhale in some more confidence before—the door opens to bright bar lights, sounds of vacuums, and indistinctive foreign language.

I use my left hand to help shade off the glare as my vision adapts to the fluorescent lights. My sight is impaired momentarily but quickly recovers while I head down into the dome-like seating. As I walk past all of the vacant spaces, empty beer bottles, cocktail cups, and over napkins—so many napkins, I can almost taste the aftermath of a Friday night.

I look at the bar. I'm stopped in my tracks as I notice the old man is no longer seated at the bar. He is gone, gone as though he were never there. Gone as though this night was all for not. The Old Man's blazer with the purple stitching is gone from the back of his stool, his black Kangol hat gone, and even his crystal rocks glass that sat on the saucer dish, all gone without a trace as if he were never there. In their place, my half-full Sazerac sits where the old man's drink would, my pink bomber jacket has taken the position of the old man's blazer, and my glass of water sits where the old man's Kangol hat sat the entire night.

Frantically I walk up to the bar looking around back and forth, frenzied by the old man's absence, mad that someone moved my things. I hope my looks will make the old man appear, walk up, or materialize out of nowhere, but no luck. Braxton walks from the other side of the bar with a rag on his right shoulder, looking at me, but he's not of my worry.

I then walk over to the far left of the bar, looking upstairs to the Moon Library, thinking the old man might have used the bathroom, but that area is blocked off; only the cleaning crew is doing their due diligence. I hear spray bottles, Cumbias playing, the hum of cleaning appliances, but no old man.

I walk around the entire bar, checking all corners and seats. Finally, I walk back over to my stool, feeling the emerald of curiosity on me. As I take my seat in yet another flummox, I decide to ask Braxton about the old man.

"Hey, Brax, what happened to the old guy I was sitting with?"

I grab my glass and sip my Sazerac whilst looking down at the old man's seat. All of my things are right here, in this seat, "my seat," but this is where the old man sat the whole night. I sip my Sazerac one more time, then reluctantly sit in my seat.

It feels weird sitting here, in this spot, for the first time all night. I begin looking around as though my looks will make something missing reappear, but to no avail. I do not believe the old man would leave without at least saying goodbye. Would he?

It was apparent that the old man and I were not going to be pen pals, and I can't imagine we would be dinner mates anytime soon, but I did expect a proper farewell, best wishes, or at the very least, we would exchange numbers; never to use them. But for the old man to leave without saying a word.

Braxton pulls the rag off his shoulder, throws it on the bar, and hastily pulls my Sazerac away. Next, he slides the glass of water in place of the Sazerac.

"What, old man?"

Braxton's perplexion is not curiosity but frustration as he places my drink underneath the bar. His movement is calm while the onyx of anger follows the Sazerac. I'm pretty fucking put off that Braxton has taken my Sazerac, so,

"Yo, w—why you take my drink?"

It's a prideful slur that receives the emerald of vexation but no drink.

"Drink some of that water, bud."

Braxton demands strong and direct. His emerald glares down at my glass of water then the emerald connects to the onyx.

"I think you've had enough tonight. DRINK water."

Braxton's words hit my ear as he pours out the rest of my Sazerac. Viewing the brownish-pink liquid makes its final descent, my onyx could leak if not for the many tears shed only moments ago.

"Ok, ok, I'll drink the water, but where's the old man?"

Braxton looks back at me, confused, shaking his head, a bit worried. He is protruding his bottom lip, biting down on his mandible jaw. Every time Braxton bites down on his jaw, the muscles on the sides of his chin flare out, pushing the red hairs of his beard out like whiskers. Finally, he throws his right hand up in exhaustion.

"Ha, what old man? What on earth are you talkin' of, brotha?"

Braxton shakes his head, suspicious of my possible inebriation, exhausted by the duality of what he believes to be a delusion and what I know to be reality.

"There was an old man sitting in this seat all night; Kangol hat, black blazer, fantastic watch; he was also drinking a Sazerac."

I'm giving Braxton details, searching for the emerald of recollection, but frustrated that he might be fucking with me. Emerald connects to onyx as Braxton stops the shake of his head.

"You know, brotha, you've been acting mental all night… I just knew I should have cut your ass off after the second Sazerac."

Braxton wipes the bar, not so much to clean it, but as a nervous tick; very Sam Malone—like he is gearing up for a real heart to heart.

"You know Malic; I never say anything when you are in here bothering my waitresses."

Braxton and I share a forced chuckle.

"I never say anything when you are harassing people about what you call "your seat," or when you and your boys are loud as all hell...."

I nod in agreement feeling somewhat embarrassed.

"And I never ban you from coming in here when you act like a drunken fool… but tonight, you were drunk, brotha…

"You ARE drunk."

Braxton leans in even deeper on the bar, ensuring what comes next will be heard over the vacuums and the background chatter.

"You keep asking about an old man, but you've been alone all night; in that very seat, "your seat." I tried warning you about having more than three Sazeracs."

Braxton proclaims as I squint, shaking my head, not wanting to believe him, but Braxton's sobriety makes me evaluate that which has not been considered; I have been drinking.

"Hey, I was ecstatic that you finally ordered a real cocktail, but when you got drunk...."

Braxton lets the emerald roll with the tilt of his head.

"You let the Sazerac take hold of ya, brotha."

Braxton's voice is authoritative, like a parent making a point after a child's mistake. I have no words because Braxton might be telling the truth. Still, I know the old man was here with me. I just know he was. Wasn't he?

"There was never an old man, just one-two many Sazeracs for a rookie drinker."

Braxton pulls back from the bar, then uses his right hand to mimic drinking, playfully teasing me. I nervously begin rotating the water glass, looking into the liquid, then I look back to Braxton.

"So you mean to tell me I spent the whole night alone instead of talking to women? That I imagined some old man? That out of nowhere I ordered a Sazerac?"

I give Braxton the stern, onyx of disbelief, but still, he nods his head.

"Yes, brotha… Yes. Even the girls wondered what the hell was wrong with ya; I just blamed it on the Sazerac."

Braxton chuckles to himself whilst wiping the bar, recalling moments of the night.

"Brax, I promise you, a wealthy man was sitting here with me, talking to me, buying me drinks. I think he was the owner or something."

The words are confident, but worry blankets Braxton's rugged, hipster-leprechaun features. Emerald searches my onyx, hoping for signs of coherence, but Braxton seems not to find what he seeks. Instead, he grabs my glass off the bar and fills it with more water and ice.

"Drink this!"

His demand has the bass of a big brother. I grab the glass from his hand then pull the cooling liquid up to my lips. Braxton is a good guy, he means well, and I have always respected him, so I do as he demands.

"Malic, brotha, you come in here most weekends, typically with your boys, occasionally with a beautiful girl, I assume you're dating. There is something there when you are with her, but you seem to be hiding from it… You know what years of bartending have shown me?"

Braxton throws words in my direction as I put my glass down, quietly shaking my head. I have no idea what he is asking, but I believe nature is rhetorical.

"Brotha, I have served thousands of patrons at bars worldwide. I have bartended at beaches, on boats, in nightclubs and restaurants, festivals and weddings, cruise ships and concerts, and all kinds of bars. The scenery changes, the drinks change, and even the music changes, but the people all stay the same."

I look to Braxton with the onyx of confusion, feeling there is no way in hell everyone is the same. He recognizes my lost look, then uses animated hand gestures to reassure me that his story has a point.

"Of course, the color of skin may be different, the language, but the reason people come to bars is always the same, from this Mad City, all the way to the other side of the world...

"People come to bars to either run away from something or find something. It's that simple, and you, my friend, are running."

Emerald peers into the onyx as I lift the glass of water to my lips. I take another nervous gulp as Braxton walks away, leaving his words in the air. He walks over to a computer, taps the screen a few times, and then prints a check. Braxton holds the check in hand, shocked by the receipt, then shakes it off. Afterward, he pulls out a billfold, places the bill inside, and walks back to me.

"You keep talking about an old man; you say he was the owner, that he was wealthy, but why do you have this bill for five Sazeracs and two Heinekens? Why didn't he pay your tab if this old man was real and wealthy?"

Braxton begins to growl with frustration, impatience, and unwillingness to hear more about the old man. I try pleading my case once more, but Braxton stops my words with a hand.

"You need to stop doing this to yourself, coming in here, drunk, running away from a relationship; running in here to drown your worries... And I'm not paying your fucking bill this time...."

Braxton throws the billfold on the bar in my direction.

"...those Sazeracs aren't cheap."

Braxton ends with a scolding look. It is surreal feeling this cold, moist, pleather billfold in hand. The billfold has recently been wiped clean, cleared of all of the liquor and dirt, wiped clean of all the night's regrets. A chill runs up my spine as I hold this black billfold in hand, trying to absorb that which I do not believe. Braxton continues wiping the bar, looking at me as I sit flabbergasted.

Was the old man just some part of my imagination, an intoxicated reaction created by Absinthe? Perhaps he was a trick of time and mind and moment? Or maybe, just maybe, the old man was something more, something more potent than touch, taste, and sound?

I open the billfold to a receipt that reads $251.96, and the weight of my jaw is more than I can bear. Wow, the cost of five Sazerac is almost more frightening than the truth—more chilling than what Braxton has said about the old man. I look down at the bill in terror, not by the cost of the drinks—which is scary as FUCK, but now I fear my mind a menace.

"Are you sure there was no old man? Are you fucking with me Brax?"

I pick the billfold up off the bar, trying to hand it back to Braxton, feeling like this might be the old man's final jape.

"This can't be the bill."

Braxton pushes the billfold back, never gripping it.

"Yeah, when you ordered the first one, I gave you the "look," especially when you ordered Woodford Reserve. But after that, you ordered so confidently. It was not my place and is never my place to argue with you about what you want. You are a big boy; you ordered a big boy drink, now pay your big boy tab."

Braxton is not budging, not joking either, and his patience has begun to dissipate.

"You see, this is a huge lesson for you. You should be at home with your beautiful woman, making her happy, making love, making a family; instead, you come in here night after night. Why?"

I hang my head as Braxton walks up closer to the bar. The vacuums in the back mean nothing; the background language, the Cumbias, all mean nothing. I look up at Braxton, giving him my full attention, much like I gave the old man.

"When you come in here, you are not talking to women or searching for new friends; most of the time, you are here wasting money, bothering my employees, or both. So often you are in here going through the motions, not really attempting to be with anyone, not really doing anything of substance."

Braxton's concerned look puts him at pause, but then he continues.

"You don't belong here, Malic. You aren't as shallow as half of the fucks who come in here, but you would like to be for some reason...

"Why is that? What are you running from?"

As did the old man Braxton is peering into the core of me, seeing things within me that I would not recognize, seeing these things that are so often ignored.

"You sound like him."

The words fall out of my mouth as I cling to the old man's stories, as I hold on to the old man's image—to the moment, as I cling onto the time I sat with the old man and the Sazerac.

"I sound like who, Malic?"

Braxton asks shortly, exasperated, not genuinely seeking my answer.

"The old man I was sitting with. T-t-the old man I was here with all night."

Words fly out of my mouth in hysteria, hoping that the sound of my voice will help Braxton believe me, but these words have an adverse effect.

"Malic, pay the bill and give me your keys."

Braxton puts his right hand out, moving his finger back and forth in the "give me" motion. He has been helpful enough to drive me home when I've been hitting the sauce too hard, and I suppose he feels tonight is another one of those instances. Reluctantly I hand my keys over—quickly, Braxton snatches them out of my hands. He then gives me this piercing gleam of emerald that stills me like a child.

"For the last time, there was no old man here with you, and yes, ownership was in the building, but he was in the kitchen all night. Our shitty chef got fired."

Braxton lets out a slight chuckle about what transpired in the kitchen.

"Look, earlier I witnessed you talking to yourself; Trixie pointed it out... but I brushed it off because Absinthe does have some properties that can play with the human mind..."

Braxton tilts his head from side to side, grinding his teeth, looking like he feels somewhat responsible.

"...I just assumed that I poured a bit more in your glass than normal, t-that you were reacting to the Absinthe."

Braxton wears the emerald of guilt; there is this subtle regret in them, but then the shake of his head puts fix to feel.

"Just put your card in here, and let's go."

Braxton holds the billfold in his hand, open, ready to receive my card for payment. I dig into my back left pocket, retrieve my wallet, then defeatedly reach in to grab out my debit card. I slap it in the billfold; Braxton closes it, then quickly walks to the end of the bar to enter the payment.

As Braxton walks off to the computer, a peculiar worry holds me. Could the old man really be some sort of reaction to the Absinthe? Or did I blackout?

The shake of my head means to shake up the voice; the voice in my head is intended to help me recollect this night; the watch, the Kangol hat, his sharp but subtle dress, the shine of his bald head, the Sazerac. The old man was a black man about 6'2" in height, with an all-white goatee, high cheekbones, and onyx-colored eyes.

Huh?

Man, that black blazer with purple lining; stylish yet subtle, minimalist chic. The old man's style could be my style; if I had the money. Shit, if I had the cash, that is how I would look, and I have always been so fond of the color purple. And there are not many men who love purple as much as I do, but the stitching on his blazer was evident proof of shared adoration.

I recall the watch, which caught my eye and stole time. I can see it now; the old man's watch, that beautiful work of timely art. The details, the sapphire face, rose gold; correction, I mean pink gold. I have always been partial to pink gold, and I will buy watches in Italy someday; I just know I will. I can see the watch on the old man's left wrist, much like I would wear my watch on the same side.

I begin rotating my water glass, thinking of the night, the old man, and its meaning. The old man also nervously circled his glass, funneling the liquid within, spinning on his thoughts. Then I see that look on his face, the look he had after I closed my eyes, after I visualized "Leggy," as though he were in the moment with me—as though I were helping him remember that which once was forgotten.

As I recall once more these pieces of a man; the purple stitching in the old man's blazer, some of the comments he made throughout the night, the watch, the stories, his ambition, his regret, the onyx color of his eyes, iI feel as though I might be mad. I sit back on my barstool, looking into the enchanted liquor shelf. The vines crawl up and twist to the top, wrapping and gripping the platinum bell. They move slow but with purpose, serpentine up to the top of the liquor shelf. The vines seem to be breathing as they grip hold of the mahogany frame, grasping the wood firmly, pulsating hard, hard, so hard the wood could suffocate—so hard the mahogany frame could burst.

"I've been where you are; I have sat in your seat...."

I hear the old man's voice again in my head; the similarities; I can listen to myself in him.

"We are not so different, you and I...."

As the old man's voice echoes in my head, I see myself in him. Onyx connects to onyx, and I am him—I feel myself sitting in his seat—my seat—sitting right here. His clothes transform into the clothes I wear—as though time has folded in half to take the old man out of existence to leave me alone at the bar.

The old man never once ordered a drink; he just had one. The old man never went to the bathroom; never interacted with anyone besides me. So when Dee came into the bar, he could not see the old man because he was never there.

Fuck!

The old man only communicated with me the entire night—he only spoke to me, just me. Not Braxton, not Trixie, not any of the beautiful waitresses or women; he only conversed with me. The old man never asked me my name; he already knew it and never tried to give me his, stating it was unimportant. The old man never gave me his name, for his name is my own—my name is his name.

Shock flows throughout my body; I begin to shake. Neurons shoot off and fire as I recall the old man's facial features and the onyx color of his eyes. Mentally I see the details of who I would become, of who I might come to be. It becomes terrible seeing your like in an unflattering light, but that like has not to become you, does it?

The old man's comments about my clothes and hair completely ripped me apart—knowing how to get under my skin. His remarks of how foolish he was, of losing his Belle, were all directed at the person he was and the person I might become. Intensely I replay this strange night, nonplussed by what unravels in my head.

No wonder the old man w—was emotionally invested in who I am. T-the weight that my relationship held on him was so r-real. My brain is beginning to skip—shuttered by the truth—frightened as though I have connected with a g-gh-ghost. I take in another deep breath to calm my beating heart. A few deep inhales, two audible sighs, then right back to the realization.

I am the person the old man wanted to outgrow—he was the person I am afraid to become. I think back to the trepidation felt when viewing the old man alone at the bar, petrified because he is me, and I was him.

The old man is the future that scares me; my biggest fear. It is not the fear of failure, not the fear of not having enough money or women, but the actual fear of being alone—the fear of not having a family.

Fear, that ultimate trepidation, that everlasting-uncanny angst of becoming the old man and the Sazerac alone at a bar. Alone with only regrets of the past as company. It is unclear if he traveled back from my future or if I moved forward from his past, but the old man was me, and if I am not careful, I might be him.

Chapter 13: Is he even Irish?

"Here you go, brotha."

Braxton slides the billfold over to me. Once again open it in disbelief as I see how much I owe. I will leave $251.96 plus the $70 as a tip; maybe this is why I never order these damn cocktails. I write the tip, sign my name whilst giving Braxton a death stare, insinuating guilt.

"All right, hurry up and sign that so we can get out of here; I have a few girls I'm meant to meet with."

Braxton comments as he scrolls through the messages on his phone. I look back at him, slide the billfold over, then chuckle.

"Ha, ha. Yeah, I bet you do, Brax… I bet you do."

Braxton grabs the billfold off the bar, opens it up, and curls his bottom lip while giving a nod of approval.

"Funny thing about you, Malic is whenever you get drunk, you fucking call me Brax, which I'm not particularly fond of, but you always tip well, which I am very fucking fond of."

Braxton walks off to input my tip into the computer system, happy with what he sees. I dwell on what the night meant, soaking in all of the lessons, contemplating what might be lost.

Illegra.

Regardless of whether the old man was real or a figment of time and mind, one thing's for sure, I can't deny my feelings for Illegra any longer, and I better shape up before I lose her.

What time is it?

Digging through my pockets makes me once again realize that I forgot my phone, so I stare off into the liquor shelf. I look deep into the enchanted liquor cabinet, remembering all of the moments that Illegra and I have shared—the times she has been there for me, the love, and the support she gives. As light glares through each bottle, I can feel all that the old man wanted me to see; all of the time, my youthful mind didn't take notice. There they are, these moments that Illegra and I have shared, the occasions more precious than money, those priceless moments when love is so apparent, but I also see my foolishness.

Braxton believes that I am drunk—incoherent, but this feeling is not that of intoxication, instead some sort of profound realization, a mental transformation into something more. My entire world feels different; this change, this moment, I feel different. The glare from each bottle is the wake-up call—the signal—the final sign for me to get my shit together, the proverbial light at the end of my dark tunnel.

Lost in a daze thinking of Illegra, I hadn't noticed Braxton coming from behind the bar. He startles me with a pat on the back.

"All right, let's get out of here; I have these two girls waiting on me."

Braxton says with his backpack strapped around his right shoulder. His bag clanks and tings with every step he takes as the bar tools move within it. I get up from my stool, sobering up with each moment, thinking of what I will say to Illegra and how I will apologize. I want to let her know how much of a fool I have been. I want to confess my love and let her know I'm no longer scared of my feelings.

"We'll go out through the side; just let me lock the front door."

It is impressive how Braxton can say the most American things but still sound Irish as fuck in other moments like his accent fluctuates. He locks the front door, then looks around the bar for some last-minute checks before speaking to a woman from the cleaning crew. I walk over to the stairs leading up to the Moon Library, peering into the skylight.

As I look up into the ivory beam of the majestic universe, I feel her power and wonder. Is there still a chance to salvage the mess that might be my relationship? Can one such as I mend the pieces of a woman's broken heart?

This entire night has sobered me to show the error of my ways, this reflection of a lost dullard, and how it all must change. Thoughts still me as I stare upstairs, into the stars, seeking answers.

"All right, brotha, let's get the fuck out of here."

Braxton and I walk through the dome-like seating, past the vacant spaces, up the few stairs leading to the bathroom, then through the third door to the kitchen. Walking through the kitchen, Braxton stops to clock out, and I patiently wait while dwelling on the night. I stand in remembrance of the lessons the old man taught me and the wise words of Braxton. It scares me to think of what I might become, of what future awaits me.

The old man is me, and I was him; my mind trails off on this thought.

As Braxton and I finally get outside, my inebriation seems too slow, like all of the learning, and everything I have heard from tonight finally settles. I want to get home to Illegra. I want to get back to her, let her know how much I care for her, how much I need her, and I want to apologize for my doltish actions. I need to get back to Illegra with no complications—no irritated bartender dropping me off, just me, my heart, and our future together.

"Hold up, brotha, let me turn off the logo."

Braxton runs off to a metal box on the side of the building, kneels, then flips off the switch. I can see "RUM" in bright green neon letters, but the banner goes dark. Even though the lights to the logo are off, I can see what the letters spell out, illuminated and assisted by the alabaster shine of the moon, "futuRUM se."

"Braxton, say brotha, what's "futurum se"?"

Braxton walks up to me, then stops to look back.

"What, you never knew the name, bud?"

I shake my head.

"Futurum se, is Latin for 'future self,' or at least I believe that's the translation."

Braxton walks past me, heading to his car; I begin to follow, then pause.

Future self?

The old man was me, and I was him.

Future self. Neurons pop off and explode in my head as what this night means flows through every atom in my body. The realization moves me, so moved I can't seem to move.

"Hey Braxton, I think I am fine, brotha. I don't need a ride home."

Braxton stops, then irritatedly turns back to me.

"I'm not too sure. I mean, you seemed pretty fucked up all night, bud. What's changed within the last few minutes?"

As Braxton's words travel from his red whiskers to my coffee-colored ears; the thoughts, the notions, the realization of Illegra, time, and love, the old man at the bar, Braxton's words, the watch, the Sazerac, all of these thoughts of my past and my future rush through me like an emotional locomotive. The fact that I want love over money, that there is much more to life than the fancy watches, the loose women, or the exotic places, all of that means nothing. The money, the life, it all means nothing without her, without Illegra. A lot has changed, and more importantly, I have changed.

This newfound sense of excitement flows through me, like the light of a new man, as though I can see what once could not be seen.

"A lot has changed, Braxton; a whole lot has changed."

Braxton looks at me closely, scratching his head in confusion; very reluctant, then I let out the phrase,

"Futurum se."

His face wrinkles and I recognize that lost look even in the dark of night. But, unfortunately, my retort has produced a flummox; it's written out all over his hipster's face.

"What?… Come on, Malic, let's get the fuck out of…."

"No, Braxton, seriously, I'm good."

Onyx connects to emerald as my direct words collide with Braxton's ears. I begin walking up to him, ready to collect my keys.

"So, you are going to tell me that in a matter of twenty minutes, you've sobered up?"

I nod my head with a very confident YES.

"Inside the bar, you were having hallucinations about an old man. You thought some old guy was going to pay your tab. You fuckin thought you were having a conversation with someone who was never there. But now, just like that, you are sober? Just like that?"

Braxton's emerald eyes, even in the moonlight, seem to pierce me, scanning for signs of intoxication.

"Shall we perform a sobriety test? Although I'm not as sober as you, I promise that I can drive the ten blocks home. Plus, I wouldn't want to be the reason you keep a threesome waiting or possibly lose it."

Speaking with not one slur of my words, I point to Braxton's phone in hand as it vibrates. He looks down at his phone, giving me a nod of slight agreement—Braxton fiddles with my keys in his left hand as he answers the text back with his right. I'm sure he is texting the women whilst weighing the options between doing what he believes to be right or letting me go.

"I mean, I shouldn't let you go, but you are a grown-ass man. Plus, I have two women waiting on me most of the night."

Braxton shrugs, put his phone in his pocket, then places his right hand on my shoulder.\

"Malic, go home, brotha. Be with your girl. Live life… Be a good man."

The weight of his words could pull my head to sand, but then emerald connects to onyx, and I'm lifted by a friend. Braxton stares deep within the gem of me, grasping my heart with sincere words and the emerald of kindness.

"One thing that I have noticed about you every time you come in, while your boys are all over women, while I'm all over women, pretty much while everyone…."

Braxton's use of animated hands helps explain the vastness of all those getting theirs.

"…gets women, you find ways to distract yourself from the riff-raff…You spend more time talking to your boys, other men, or even on nights like tonight, and you spend time alone. Now originally, I thought you might have been playing for the other team…"

He mimics the motion of giving a handjob, keys in hand, with jingle playing to gesture.

"…you know, putting from the rough, but then I saw your woman and how you were around her. Life isn't about the women you sleep with, brotha, or the parties you go to…You're not missing shit.

"Ok, sure, I'm about to go and have an amazing threesome with two American girls that love my accent. They like the accent… Women dig it, regardless of how dumb I might be or how dumb I feel they are. These girls will do anything I tell them to do because I will say that European girls do this and that, or I will act like it is my first threesome. They will believe me because I'm the foreign guy that is way better than Americans."

Braxton shrugs with a devilish smirk that gleams in the vanilla beam of night, then continues.

"The whole point is this, brotha, don't let something beautiful like what you have to go because you want to fit in, the fear of missing out, or because you are trying to hang with the boys.

"The boys, the bars, and even the babes will always be there, but a chance at love, real love, when that comes around, you better grab it."

Like a wise hipster-leprechaun, Braxton hits me with the last lesson of the night, a little treasure of the mind, before he hands me my keys.

"You drive safe, bud, and I'll go have sex with these American broads."

We both chuckle and give a dab before Braxton walks off. As he drives away, a few thoughts occur to me. First and less critical, Braxton might only have that accent to bed American girls, which has only come to my attention tonight. Second, he's right about everything. Even if his wise leprechaun act is all a farce, he is correct, as was the old man correct in his many assessments.

Getting back to Illegra's Mini Cooper, I feel all of the lessons this night, and I couldn't be more excited to get home. I hop in the car, put the keys in the ignition, then look into the rearview mirror. The onyx-colored eyes of a young man who is still learning looks back, one who, although he is not perfect, these onyx-colored eyes of his are starting to see life in a more vivid picture.

Turning the key, starting the roar of the mini but powerful engine, I begin to drive out of the now-empty parking lot, with only the van of the cleaning crew that remains. The music blast loud; Kendrick Lamar raps, and quickly I turn the stereo off. Right now, I want to live in my thoughts, with no distractions as I drive home to Illegra.

Thoughts from the beginning flow through me; the nostalgia of how it all begins, the woman Illegra, and the man I am. The night that Illegra and I met, I worked at a club; she was partying with her girls. I was in my section cleaning the recently empty table when I spotted her. I will never forget how I felt when I saw her, how the entire night stopped, and how she stood out amongst thousands. She wore a short black skirt and a lavender tank top with black suspenders. Oh, her skin shined. She looked like a tall, stunning, black-haired Aphrodite shot straight down from Olympus; this godly glow.

I knew that I had to drop everything to meet this enthralling woman from the moment I saw her. Leaving my section in the middle of cleaning a table, I knew nothing could stop me as I followed her through the dance floor. Never before had I felt such magnetism as I left my area in complete disarray to chase down this blue-eyed goddess. She stole my attention entirely. Never have I before that night, or any night thereafter, felt in such away. When she looked back at me as I approached her, the universe and my heart stopped; the universe changed forever.

The fog of the memory has me; these passionate moments float in my air and mind. Approaching the apartment complex, my heart stops--it stops once again, just as it stopped the night I met Illegra.

Fear.

Fright loiters within me; this woman of my dreams, I have hurt her, and now I fear what might become of our otherwise unbecoming relationship.

From the car, I look up at the window that leads to the living room. The lights are off, but the flicker of the television screen leaves me hopeful. I turn off the car, turn off the lights, then sit for a moment.

I was such a dick, and I have left her alone tonight and on many nights. I've chosen friends over her, work over her. I wouldn't change my relationship status on the off chance that I would meet someone new, leaving the "door" open for other romance. I have flirted with other women, kissed them, and have been a terrible, doltish man to Illegra. I don't deserve her; she deserves much better than this, but I must try. After all, I have done, I owe Illegra a better man.

Illegra has time and time again been there for me, uplifting me; she has been my rock, the family when I have had none, and most of all, Illegra has loved me even when loving myself seemed impossible.

Her patience, sense of humor, and intelligence, even before looks, make Illegra a woman that I am lucky to know, let alone be with; Illegra has been a godsend—a deity—an enchanted being shot down from Olympus to make a mere mortal more.

Illegra has never lost faith in me, even though I have lost jobs, my difficulty with emotions, and my overall doltish immaturity. She puts up with me.

I grip the steering wheel not because I will be leaving but to grab hold of these strong feelings. I never expected this night to be so profound and enlightening, but here I am. I was expecting the end of my—our relationship, calling it quits; now, this feels like the beginning of my true feelings.

Maybe that's what this is all about; the old man, the Sazerac, the heart to heart with Braxton, even running into Chris. I release my grip from the wheel as life becomes one realization, one clear picture. Reclining in the driver's seat, exhaling all of my emotions, this recognition that I have been running from said emotions calms me as I prepare to be confronted with them at full force. Never have my feelings been so on-point and cohesive, so focused on love, and I can't wait to let them out. I can not wait to share this feeling with my beautiful Belle.

My past has convinced me that hiding my emotions makes me strong, more independent, and a lone wolf, but that can no longer be who I am. I open the door and take yet another deep breath before getting up. As I take what seems to be the longest walk to my front door, I picture Illegra running into my arms, and I twirl her dramatically like the "Notebook" or some "rom-com" from the late 90s' or early 2000s'. We confess our undying love; we passionately kiss, decide that we will never leave each other's side, the movie slows, and then enter baby or babies, big house, and our happy montage in the end credit scene of our romantic movie.

One could only wish that love were ever so simple.

Chapter 14: Danger Zone

My body begins to change temperature, and as I reach for the front doorknob, a chill comes over me. Goosebumps develop, the hair on my neck stands tall as Mutumbo, I fidget, and just like that, I'm frightened as a boy. This feeling of meeting Illegra for the first time sends my whole body into trembles; as my hands begin to sweat, they shake a little, and my stomach feels as empty as the parking lot of the futuRum Se. This electrical current that can only be called fear races from my brain to my tingling fingertips as the house key slides into the nob.

My rom-com fantasy would come to fruition in a perfect world, my love would jump directly into my arms, and our love would be whole. She would love me, I would love her, and life would be wonderful, but as the door opens, the reality is less rom-com fantasy, more debaucherous sleepover.

The flat screenplays old episodes of Law and Order: SVU; there are pizza boxes, one pepperoni; barely touched, the other anchovies and jalapenos with one slice left. This half-full bottle of merlot stands next to two empty bottles of unspecified red and shot glasses that sit next to a three-quarters full bottle of Stoli, blueberry vodka, which makes me swallow some courage. Snoring like a moose in winter is Marla, Illagra's best friend.

Damn, this place looks like a tornado of male-bashing; Tasmanian she-devils had an orgy of hate and destruction throughout the night, and in my living room no less. This scene is the aftermath of an all-night heart to heart, fueled by booze, bad pizza, and bags of Hershey's kisses. And I mean like a lot of Hershey's kisses; wrappers are all over the floor, and on top of Marla, gold, silver, even some foil wraps with stripes. There will be some trace of ice cream somewhere; Illegra devours that shit by the gallon when she is pissed.

But this sight of Marla sprawled out on the couch; purple lips, pizza sauce on her face, anchovy hanging from her bottom lip, hair disheveled, with her vomit-colored tank top, bright orange yoga pants, sauce stains, wine drips, and now slabber, all which accentuates her sloven look; this sets the tone for what my room will look like and Illegra's presumably state. Although Illegra is not a lush, the horror of what awaits me sends a different sense of caution up my spine; this fear of the final confrontation.

Walking through the disaster that once was my living room, climbing over empty bottles, clothes, and pizza boxes, angst takes me before almost killing myself on one of Illegra's heels. I survive, luckily, and without a skip of Marla's stertorous breathing.

Before getting to the half-cracked bedroom door, I take a deep breath like a kid scared to be confronted by his parents, peering through the door's crack, hoping for some signs of safe entry. Unfortunately, I can't see much; I don't hear her, only Ice T in the background, clearly detailing the importance of a crime scene. Walking into the room, I notice the bathroom light is on and clothes all over the place, like more clothes than usual. It seems as though Illegra was in the process of packing her things, then maybe called Marla for help. I look over to the bed where Illegra lays with the blanket covering her, back to me, clearly asleep. Remaining mindful of the noise, I make my best impression of a tip-toeing ninja as I enter the room.

I probably would have stumbled through the mess on any other night, flopping myself on the bed next to her, but tonight is different. On this night, I walk in as quiet as a mouse, careful and courteous, cautious not to wake the lioness. I close the door, but not completely shut, in fear of the sound it might make. Immediately after, I walk into the bathroom and once again leaving the door cracked, not making much of a sound. I take another deep breath of relief before catching the onyx in the mirror.

For a moment, the person I used to be, attempts to take over as I stare onyx to onyx. My fear of confrontation sets in by trying to get me to run, a defense mechanism against emotion—against honesty, a foolish defense created by my doltish fear. Running from my feelings is what got me here, but that is not the person I want to be; that is not the man Illegra deserves.

Much like Jekyll, I feel my foolish Hyde trying to take over, intoxicated by fear, crippled by confusion. This salty taste in my mouth, fear, like warm ocean water—like the regurgitation of regret, of foolishness, as though I am ready to spit up the person I no longer am. This fluid drips from the side of my mouth, slipping, hoping to escape, hoping to wash my mouth of this doltish angst.

I spit into the sink, ridding my lips of that taste, my past, my past-future, and the old man. I look back up into the mirror as onyx once again connects to onyx.

There is so much I want to say to Illegra, so many parts of me I want to let loose, to let her know that I can be the man she needs and that she is the only woman I will ever need. I just want to let her know I love her. Looking down into this sink, I am thinking, dwelling, wondering; then I turn the faucet on to wash my face, but then spot my phone next to the sink.

As a parent who has lost their child at the mall, I grab my phone with such urgency, such excitement, then quickly open it. I put in my passcode to see that I have 30 text messages, 5 missed calls, 6 Instagram notifications, and 10 Facebook pops. Next, I check my text messages.

10:40pm[Alex]

Hit me up, brotha…ASAP

Crazy turn of events…

10:45pm [Dee & Alex]

Alex- Yo, not gonna make it out?

Alex- I'll explain later…

11:15pm[Dee & Alex]

Dee- Fellas, I'm staying in wit o'girl tonight…. No Rum

Alex- Actually me too…

Dee- No shit?

Dee-Yo Alex, are you still wit o'gurl from last week?

Alex-

Dee- Are you fucking kidding me?

Alex-Yea, we been fucking all damn week, my piece is raw!!

Dee- Shit I'm working on the "cut up" as well.

Alex- Who you wit?

Dee- Breezy from the bowling alley…

Alex and Dee's ridiculous texting continued for about another hour and a half—two hours, full of dick jokes, sex gifs, and horny cartoon memes. Those guys can turn anything into a gif war, and they are always ready to clown.

There are quite a few text messages from Illegra, but I am not ready to see her words just yet. So instead, I check Marla's text. Marla has left this super threatening and detailed text; something about eating my balls at a bar mitzvah, in front of Jewish kids, and kosher sausage; very classy as she always can be. However, her text was very detailed and scary; Marla can be a frightening woman given the right or wrong circumstances. Everything she needed to say in this one detailed message, and I now fear Marla a little more, but then my thoughts go back to Leggy.

"Leggy," that's what she's saved as in my phone. Since grade school and even on the runway, this sobriquet has stalked Illegra. It is a name that family members and close family now use, the name that I use to soften her up. Typically I receive eye rolls, jabs to the gut, and sometimes a smirk. Leggy, the green bubble on my phone that indicates unread messages—the tab that I hit to open up all of her texts from this strange night. Leggy.

10:35pm [Leggy]

Of course, you would run and have fun at your fucking bar.

10:46pm[Leggy]

Really…No reply?

You are such a fucking coward.

10:52pm [Leggy]

Ugh, i cant wait for you to fucking grow up. TEXT ME BACK!!!!

11:15pm [Leggy]

Babe, can we please just talk…

I don't want to put pressure on you but I think we should talk about this. This is serious. Please call me.

11:35pm [Leggy]

I owe it to myself to be treated better but regardless of what happens after tonight, I will be better, but at least let me know that you are ok.

12:04am [Leggy]

Good…Good…Go ahead and throw everything we have or will have a way…Go

12:25am [Leggy]

COWARD!!! Fucking coward.

12:45am[Leggy]

I'm taking your shit, and I'm burning it. I'm taking all of these fucking Jordan's I've bought you, and I'm burning them.Then I am getting the fuck out of here.

1:15am[Leggy]

Seriously babe just text me.

2:30am[Leggy]

Well, I've gone through a range of emotions. The truth is that I know it's tough for you to express your feelings. I know that your past has made you tough, but you can open up to me.

2:32am[Leggy]

I do love you; you mean the world to me, but at the same time, I feel I owe it to myself to be treated much better; I know being forthright about your emotions is not your most acceptable quality, but just let me know you care.

2:34am[Leggy]

Text me back, so I know you aren't being a drunken fool. I promise I will be here, maybe not as your girl, but I will be here

for you, even when you are a

stupidface....

2:37am[Leggy]

Please be safe, babe.... I don't care about the Facebook status.

2:40am[Leggy]

come home.... I just want you to be safe and come home... I care for you, babe, and I just want to know you are safe.

Even after I have been a dick, after leaving to go to a bar where she knows I will meet women, drink, and act like a damn fool, the one thing she cares about is my safety. My well-being is her biggest concern, even after I have acted like an immature prick. All Illegra wants is for me to be safe even after an argument.

Looking back up into the mirror, I shamefully stare into myself. What am I doing to this amazing woman?

I don't want to be with anyone else; I don't need anyone else; I don't enjoy anyone else's company; hell, I barely get along with anyone else besides maybe Dee and Alex.

I look at my phone, enter the passcode, then hit the Facebook book app. I scroll through the monotonous post, the slut-shaming, the annoying screenrants, and gym shots before hitting the icon to get to my profile page. Of course, I could have gone directly to my profile, but it is always fun to like a couple of gifs along the way before getting to my feed, that or I just fear what comes next.

Once on my profile, I tap the edit tab, then scroll down to details. As I scroll down past my work, my education, the current city I live in, finally comes relationship status. Next, I tap the pencil icon that will edit my status. The current status choice reads single; directly under the "single" tab reads "in a relationship."

Stargazed by the words "in a relationship," it's funny how old habits die hard. Considering I have always been single, changing the status seems more complicated than it should be, a severe case of "FOMO," but I snap out of it and then hit the tab.

After hitting the tab, a place where you write the name of the person you are in the relationship with pops up, so I type in her name; Illegra Russo. To my surprise, a little message pops up that says it will await the other party's approval before finalizing the update. Sure it is a little off-putting seeing this pop-up, but I still feel somewhat accomplished. It is strange how I feel like I've grown just a bit by pressing a few buttons. I'll wait until the morning to give Illegra the great news, seeing as how she is sleeping.

This strong dauntless feel has me as I slowly and quietly get undressed. I did it; I did what Illegra wanted and what the old man wanted; I made Leggy my girl, just like Braxton suggested. I then sneak out of the bathroom, leaving my clothes on the floor. Before turning off the bathroom light, I make sure to visualize my path to the bed so that I can be quiet enough not to wake her and so I don't kill myself walking through the danger zone that has become our room.

I've laid out my path, and I'm ready for the mission. I begin tip-toeing over to the bed using the flicker of the television as a guide. Once at the bed, I lightly lift the blanket, hoping to slide in undetected.

First, I slip my left leg into the bed, carefully sit my buttocks on the mattress, then slide in. No movement from Illergra's end, and I am almost home free. Lastly, I pull my right leg in, then gently lay my head down on the pillow. I send out a soft but broken sigh of relief, feeling both safe and accomplished, and then I close my eyes.

"So, did you have fun tonight?"

Chapter 15: The Love of my Life

The DJ orchestrating my heart cranks the BPMs up as I hear that raspy voice. Onyx connects to the ceiling as a sudden fright kicks my fight or flight into high gear, but I want to stay this time around. Illegra pulls the cord to the lamp on her nightstand, illuminating the room, shining light all over the mess, a bright reminder of what my foolishness has created.

This is it; no running, silly excuses, bars, old man or bartenders, selfie-taking girls, cat-calling ebony men--no bachelorette girls, and no Sazerac. Now it is just me, Illegra, and this inevitable conversation. She rolls over, sits up, then leans back on the headboard. This crestfallen air and her woebegone expression hurt my heart, but still, I turn to join her.

As I am prepared to confess my undying love, I admit I was not ready for this, not now, but here we are, yet something stops me. I have never seen Illegra broken, so beset; her dishevelment is foreign to me. Looking at a mess of my creation, I can only feel regret at this moment, and my words will not form.

"So?"

Illegra calmly asks, not looking at me. My eyes drift over to a pint of "Ben and Jerry's" salted caramel core on her nightstand, an uncommon flavor for her. It is never a good sign when Leggy does something out of the ordinary; even this change of ice cream creates caution in me.

"I-I needed to clear my head."

My feeble reply receives frustrated air, not words, just pushed breath, signifying her disappointment.

"You spent quite a bit of time in the bathroom; everything ok?"

Illegra pairs her side-eye with this subtle inquisition, calm, but words that still rattle each ear.

"You men always sneak into the house and into bed when you know you're in the wrong. You think you're so slick."

Illegra shakes her head, smacks those beautiful lips, and I know it's on. Once the words "you men" fall out of her mouth, I know I'm in for a wallop. "You men" is the verbal equivalent to a kick in the nuts.

"You men" is usually followed by a list of faults and fuck-ups, problems, and guilt-ridden premonitions. "You men " means she has hit her wit's end, and I have fallen into the same category as every other Joe. Illegra never compares me to other men; typically, I am nothing like them, but that all changed, and I became like every other man.

It is hard to admit, but I deserve every moment of this, don't I? Has not my actions; actions which have caused emotional harm, actions that have forced such a reaction, should I not, at the very least, suffer but a moment of emotional discomfort? Does not Illegra deserve this time to clear her air and speak her peace? Don't I owe her at least that?

"You men."

Illegra shakes her head.

"You men think women are stupid enough not to hear your silly asses stumbling in, trying to be quiet."

Illegra looks to me with the sapphire of cynicism and disgust, the same look that grown women give stupid little boys. The awkwardness is palpable, but the unease is so unbearable that it stinks. My palms sweat, my heart is bumping, yet Illegra remains calm. I am cautious not to provoke her; she fears I will flee, so we sit, impatient but quiet.

The same way hunters are taught not to make eye contact with a predator is how I handle our conversation's beginning moments. I have learned not to arouse the lion within an Italian woman or any woman, so I stay quiet even though I want to wrap my arms around her and kiss her. Even though I want to make love to her and show her what my love can and should be. Instead, I sit with my fingers interlocked, twiddling my thumbs, awaiting Illegra's next word.

"Well, you don't seem drunk, so hopefully, this will not go on deft ears."

She looks over to me as my head hangs down, looking at my fingers. As a kid about to be grounded, I'm hopeless compared to what comes next, fearful of what might transpire. Illegra gathers the right amount of saliva to speak, takes a quick breath, then starts.

"You know when you leave me to go drinking—when you don't answer your phone all night, when you are out with the boys, running away from confrontation, you hurt me."

Her lip vibrates with disappointment, yet still, she speaks calmly—a calmness attained from a long night of crying.

"I know babe, and I'm so...."

Illegra puts her right index finger up, stopping me in my speech. No yelling, no frustration, just one finger to shut me up.

"You don't get to call me babe; you don't get to speak. You are going to sit here and listen to every word I have to say. No running this time."

I nod my head in agreement, but Illegra's calm nature worries me. My mother always warned that a calm woman is a calculated woman, and those women are dangerous. So even though Illegra sounds cool and calm, I feel the heat in the room, the pressure, this constructed unease created by a doltish boy.

FUCK, I wish I could break the tension by telling her that I love her, that I need her, but at the same time, I owe her this. Illegra deserves to speak, and I owe her and our relationship to listen. So quietly, I sit.

"All night, I've been here asking myself these things, running circles in my mind, driving myself fucking crazy."

She looks over to the right at me; I look back. My onyx reads apologetic, but her sapphire lacks patience, a precursor to arms crossed. Illegra holds no more composure for my daftness; she isn't willing to hear the nonsense that might spill from my lips. I feel cornered by her resolve; an itch of flight hits me, then I look back to Illegra.

"Do you know what I asked myself?"

I begin to open my mouth to answer, but once again, Illegra holds her index finger up with a shake of her head, reassuring me that my words are not welcomed.

"I ask myself why I'm here? Why do I do this to myself? I asked myself why I put so much effort into a man—into a BOY that could give a shit about me?"

Illegra's face reads clear as a morbid picture book, full of distress, defeat, and disappointment, but her words crawl out patiently. At this moment, I can't attempt to tell her how I feel; how could I? What words are there to say? How can I change that which I have so foolishly created?

Illegra continues.

"You know all my friends told me when you lost your job that I should leave you? They told me that supporting you and Dee was a mistake; they said it would be the end of us. Others even told me that you weren't worth a pot to piss in. Are they right?"

Illegra stares at me, searching for answers and one last reason to stay, but I go blank. Doubt heats my face, my stomach begins to growl, and I become lost, lost in her words, the night, and the regret of all my past transgressions.

Am I worth her trouble? Maybe "they," whoever they are, might be right? And it is this critical moment that makes me ask; am I the pot or the piss?

Illegra smacks her lips, gets out of bed, then begins moving about the room. Getting out of bed is a sign of disgust; she doesn't want to sit next to me, and me going blank in my words has only pushed her further away.

After getting up out of bed, Illegra takes the rubber band from her left wrist, then calmly fashions her satin mess into a ponytail. Ready for war in all black LuLuLemon Illegra scares the hell out of me. Typically she sleeps either naked or in a nightgown, but tonight is a much different night. However, when she puts her hair into a ponytail, I hold my breath. I always brace myself when Illegra puts her hair back, good or bad.

Currently, Illegra seems calm enough to kill. Her demeanor is more terrifying than a crazed woman yelling and throwing tantrums, more freight inspiring than a woman with knives. Yet, she's as calm as a lioness stalking her prey.

In a blink of my eyes, I see a flash of the old man. He sits at the bar, alone, with only a Sazerac and his regrets to keep him company. It is a vision that creates momentary goosebumps, this a frigid feeling like walking out of the sun and into a freezer. The heat in the room is nothing compared to that chill—the cold chill of loneliness. And then, I snap myself out of the daze, then hear Illegra's voice.

"Over the past year, I have paid your rent and supported you as you pursue this dream of yours, all the while allowing you to treat me like some silly bitch…"

Illegra catches a tear on her left pinky nail.

"… Who knows what women you are sleeping with? What shit are you bringing home?"

Her voice cracks as if she caught the cry in her throat, stopping herself before showing how she feels inside.

"I have Chris of all fucking people calling me, letting me know that you are at the bar all over, women? I began to...."

That flash fucker! I throw my hands up in disgust, interrupting her.

"Chris said what?!"

I ask, hoping the heat of my words will plead honestly; my gaze is so intense I hope to implant my truth, then I think of the old man. He was right, and I can't fucking believe my ears. Of course, Chris called her; of course, that flash fucker would try making his move. Quickly I crawl to the foot of the bed to stop Illegra from pacing and to calm her heavy breathing. She won't let me touch her, but her pacing has stopped. I look deep into her, wanting to know what lie was told. She slows her breathing, then continues.

"Chris messaged me around midnight asking if we had broken up. He said you were all over some woman, and your hands we—were everywhere."

Tears escape the sapphire before she can retrieve them. Her voice breaks entirely at the end, and I can feel the crack of her heart. I shake my head, furious at the lie, then grab Illegra by her waist to pull her in close. I pull her to where she stands between my legs, then look at her. Onyx connects to sapphire, emphasizing every ounce of my truth.

"Leggy…"

She gives me a sharp look; eyebrow raise, bottom lip curls, nostrils flare, and a half head tilt. Illegra has never liked the nickname that has followed her since childhood, but I use it as a weapon to lighten her mood and soften her up.

"…now I have been a fool; there is no denying that, but I would never cheat on you and never have. That fool Chris just wants you for himself; he'll say anything to make you his again. You are a trophy to him, that's all."

She pushes my hands off of her and then steps back.

"But isn't that the reason you don't want me? Isn't that the whole reason for staying single so that you can justify flirting with other women just to feel less guilty? Isn't that your whole stitch, the hip single guy, that gets all of the girls?"

Damn, I can't deny the truth of Illegra's words. Fuck she hit the nail on the head with that one. We as men won't make relationships official to alleviate our guilt or some other nonsensical reason. We stay single for as long as possible to sow our royal oats and be with various partners guilt-free. Call it fuckboy logic, and Illegra has just pointed out every crooked screw.

"While you were out, I decided that I will leave you."

Illegra's words glide into each ear, and my heart stops, dreams shatter, and still, she continues.

"I decided that I am going to get my shit, take my name off the lease, and move in with Marla...."

Illegra points out to Marla in the living room, and her voice begins to rise. She's not shouting, but that calm demeanor she started with has slipped away.

"I was going to burn your favorite basketball jersey, throw some of the Jordan's out the window, grab my shit and leave, but I decided to give you a piece of my mind first."

This moment should be when I stop her and confess my love, but I can't get a word in edgewise. My mouth has not the power nor the courage to form the right words.

"I realized tonight that I..."

Illegra uses her right index finger to point inward into her chest.

"...am A Fucking Catch."

The subtle bass in her voice combines with the phlegm from her weeping, distorting her words, adding animation to emotion.

"I will never take Chris back no matter how much he calls me or bad mouth's you, and it doesn't matter if you were all over some bitch tonight. What does matter is that you left."

I am shaking my head, looking down into my lap, hearing her words but frightened by what it means. Illegra walks over and grabs me by the chin with her index finger and thumb, cupping my face--forcing eye contact.

"You left me here, alone. You left me after I said that I would leave you if you did. You fucking left as if that meant nothing—as if you didn't need me."

She aggressively lets go of my chin, throwing my face away from her. My head drops, and my brain rattles from the force of her gravity.

"Well, I don't need you, Malic, and I don't need this shit. So I hope you got what you needed out of tonight. I hope tonight was worth leaving me here."

Illegra states, very matter of fact, completely done with me.

"But it was."

I stand up. Illegra's look of shock almost breaks her spirit as I stand with a massive smile on my face.

"Tonight, something amazing happened to me that I can't even begin to explain, but I'll try."

The baffled look on her face wrinkles the brow, and she's left in a flummox.

"It was worth it?"

Illegra asks, tilting her head, confused. I nod with a shit-eating grin as I grab her by her upper arm close to her shoulders.

"Yes."

Onyx connects to sapphire, and I'm staring deep into the iris of the woman I love.

"Tonight, I was confronted by someone, and I spent my whole night with this person."

I want to talk about the old man, but I recall the old man never existed, or will never exist, or was a figment of my imagination, some trick of time forcing me to see that life. Either way, it is too confusing to explain, plus the last thing I need is Illegra thinking I'm crazy while professing my undying love.

"Oh, so you were all over some bitch?"

Quickly I realized the delivery was ill-prepared, but I'm fast to recover.

"No."

I grab her by the arms to stop her from throwing a fist. Illegra has brimstone in her, and all that calmness was only the preheating of a scorching oven.

"No, I was confronted by myself—by a version of myself that I never want to exist. He was a time remnant of a person I never want to become, of a person lost, and alone."

Illegra looks at me with the sapphire of perplexity, and I might just lose her. I let her go and stepped back. I hope that I can explain. I pace while Illegra stands still, right in front of the flickering television, waiting for my words. I am pacing, not out of frustration or anger, more like a person who has discovered something groundbreaking. I can't find the words; my hands twitch. I'm completely filled with excitement but also damn nervous. The overwhelming rush of the night, the old man, the Sazerac, Braxton, the "Rum," futurum se, like ripples in the ocean, the entirety of this strange night and beyond, crashes throughout my head. My brain waves crash and flow with such force that I decided it would be best to sit Illegra down on the bed and explain it all. I grab her by the forearm, walk her back to the bed, then set her down.

Where do I start without sounding like a madman? I put my hands to my mouth, almost to mimic praying, but I'm slowly gathering my thoughts. I don't want to lose her along the way; I have to be careful to explain the night so Illegra feels how much I love her.

"I want you to know everything I do; I honestly do it for you. You are my princess...."

Illegra puts her hand up.

"Don't call me princess or imply that I am a princess. I fucking hate that misogynistic, prance playing bullshit.."

I raise my hands up to calm her, get down on my knees, and crawl between her legs.

"Belle... My Belle, my love. I love you...."

Words from my mouth melt to her liking; she knows I mean it.

"Belle? Now, why the fuck would you call me "Belle"?"

She snaps at me, both frustrated and bemused by my sporadic diction.

"Because "Belle" is not a princess, but prettier and smarter than all of the rest, just like you, babe."

For the first time tonight, she gives me a smirk, and for a moment, I see it; that spark, the love that only Illegra and I share.

"That's fair; I can accept that."

The girl from the "Bricks" comes out when she is cute, this twang of city life, her verbal animation.

"I always did like "Belle," you know, but saying sweet things won't help you much."

Illegra gives me a sharp look. The next wall will not easily crumble, but I must try.

"My "Belle," I have loved you for a long time…"

She rolls her eyes, not entirely convinced; still, I continue.

".. Tonight, when I was at the "Rum," I was confronted with myself, con-confronted by a version of myself. This version of me lived a life without you, and that sight was horrifying. Yet, everything that I have done, everything that I do, is not to lose you, quite the contrary."

I grab Illegra's hands and then kiss both of them. How smooth her skin feels on my lips, how soft, how warm they are, and how beautiful her porcelain hands look cupped within my chocolate fingers.

"It was worth it for me to go to the bar tonight and see what my life would be like without you. It was worth it for me to see the man I would become without you."

I am shaking with emotion; Illegra looks at me with the sapphire of caution. She is startled by how forthright I have become, unsure of what this gesture means.

"And it was worth it for me to see myself as an older man alone, at the bar; a man who had all the money, cars, houses, women, and places, but it was nothing without you. It will be nothing without you. Not now. Not fifty years from now. Not ever."

She has a smirk on her face partnered with a cautionary raise of her brow. Light tears run down her face as we grip hands, locked sapphire to onyx, with both of our emotions out on the floor.

"What does this all mean? I'm still not your girlfriend. These words, all of this gesture, still means nothing."

Illegra lets go of my hands.

"50 years from now? All of the money, the houses, the cars? All of the WOMEN?"

When Illegra says women, there is a powerful emphasis on that mini tantrum. She sounds like an angry mob wife ready to "chop my balls off;" full "Real housewives of Jersey" style.

"What makes this different from any other apology? Huh!"

Illegra's sapphire pierces the onyx, unsatisfied, almost madder than before, then her arms cross. I stand up and move from between her legs. I walk over to my nightstand, grab my phone, crawl on the bed over to her nightstand, grab her phone, and then bring them back to her.

First, I hand her my phone as I get back down on my knees and crawl back in between her legs. I shake my head in disbelief with a smile on my face.

"If the boys could see me now," I say aloud to myself but knowing she could hear. What a doltish organization of words that only attracts her cold stare.

"M-my-my passcode on my phone is your birthday and always has been. 061284"

I want to show excitement but fear its prematureness, so I look down at the phone in her alabaster hand.

"Open up your Facebook app."

I instruct her as she looks down at her phone.

"I left my phone here all night, but as soon as I got back, I tried to change my status, but I need one thing…."

She looks back up at me; excitedly, I look at her.

"… I need you to accept the relationship."

Illegra looks down at her phone, trembling with excitement and tears running down her face, but she still shakes her head, neglecting my gesture.

She gently puts her phone face down on the bed then hands me my phone, pushing it directly into my chest. She is sobbing, not a full-out ball, but her sniffles echo my head. I look over at her phone, confused, holding my phone to the pulse of my heart.

I knew she would be happy about this; I just knew it. We should be making up, kissing, and prompt to incredible sex. I'm stunned, heartbroken; this isn't going as planned—it's not going well at all; then Illegra's harsh tone breaks our pause.

"As always, you are missing the point. It's not about the status on Facebook or the passcode to your phone. I want the passcode ro here, DUMMY."

Illegra puts her hands aggressively on me for the first time in our relationship; sure, she has thrown punches, broken dishes, and burned clothes, but she has never physically harmed me. Illegra points her index finger into my chest, liable to carve my heart out—hard enough to break a nail. As she does this, it reminds me of a moment with the old man and something he said; Illegra continues.

"And you just changing your passcode, updating your relationship status, it all just feels forced."

Illegra shakes her head, I close my lids, defeated, and the old man sits. The old man sits in my darkness and so sips his Sazerac. His skin cracks from the liquor and his body is becoming frailer, more depleted, more defeated. The old man's blood, life, and time are all hooked up to the Absinthe fountain.

"Remember the price."

A voice echoes. I look closer at the old man only to see his time flow into the fountain as it drips.

"It drips ever so rhythmically, almost hypnotizing, isn't it?"

Perhaps the last traces of Absinthe coursing through my veins echoes my voice.

'Drip.'

"Remember the price."

The old man's voice seems to mold into mine; his face and features all flow intertwined until finally, I am the old man sitting at the bar.

'Drip'

Each drop—each drip sizzles as I think of the old man, as I think of myself, alone, at the bar, talking about the price that young boys never want to pay. I recall he spoke of love as the ultimate prize; I remember him pointing to an indention in my chest, the same indentation, the same pain that Illegra has caused. The old man never clarified its price; he only said it was the price no young buck was willing to pay—a price for a prize, the ultimate prize.

The thought stills me, the vision; Illegra starts to crawl back to the headboard. My recollection has only added to her frustration as she climbs away from me. While my relationship drifts away, never to return, it all finally makes sense, and I explode off the floor.

"I remember the night my life changed forever…"

I begin to walk around the bed slowly.

"… it was about two summers ago at a little club you loved going to."

I say as she sits at the headboard, not amused but listening. Her arms are crossed, and the sapphire glimmers.

"I remember the night we met Malic."

She says short; I nod and continue.

"I remember seeing you walking through the dance floor, that skirt, those legs, the black suspenders, that fierce walk…"

I click my tongue on the roof of my mouth and pucker my lips as I recall how show-stopping she was.

"Everyone said you looked like Kate Beckinsale."

She looks back with a bit of bash; I nod.

"Yeah, and I remember letting them know Kate couldn't eat your shit if she tried."

Illegra has both a look of disgust and flattery; we both laugh. With my arms and hands as animation tools, I continue peeling away at the hard shell of Illegra.

"I remember leaving my section to get a glimpse of the woman who stole the night, thinking that after years of working at this club, I had finally found someone to steal my thunder...."

The insinuation of my good looks hopes to navigate a lighter mood; I hope to remind her of how playful we can be.

"...fantasizing that I had finally found my match, someone to match my beauty."

I brush my right hand down my face as I walk over to her side of the bed, displaying my look as a model would, playfully showcasing my features. Illegra always loves when I play arrogant, as she knows my true nature. I sneak closer to her.

"You had that pixie hair cut, those blue eyes that could pierce diamonds, legs so long that Victoria wished she had your secret; I had to have you."

I sit, scooting closer, and closer with each word. Getting through to Illegra might be possible as she drops her crossed arms. Crossed arms are the female defense pose, and I am like Steve Erwin in the wild right now, hoping to move carefully in the retrieval of love I might have lost.

"But you know when I fell in love with you?…"

Rhetorically I ask, looking into the coal of her breathtaking eyes.

"It wasn't the first date when you cried during Star Wars, or even the third date when you whooped my ass at Top Golf, or even our fifth date when you cooked me the best cavatelli pasta, and afterward you ravished me on the kitchen table,…"

She puts her hand to her face, trying to stop herself from blushing.

"…,but it was our sixth date, the date at that fancy burger spot; if there is even such a thing. But the moment when my friend Stephanie popped out of nowhere taking a huge bite out of my burger…."

Illegra covers her mouth and then begins to shake her head, holding herself back from laughing.

"…You were so mad at her for taking a bite of my burger, you said, "Hey bitch.."…"

Illegra uncovers her mouth to finish the sentence.

"Hey, bitch, who the fuck do you think you are taking a bite of my man's burger like that?"

The explosive connection of onyx to sapphire teleports us back to that night. We both begin laughing, with Illegra laughing so hard that the fluid in her eyes becomes hilarious tears.

"O, I wanted to kill that bitch."

She lets out her past frustration as I nod in agreement, grinning from ear to ear.

"Remember, I grabbed you to the side, and I…"

Illegra cuts me off before I can finish.

"You begged for me to apologize to that silly fucking bitch."

She shakes her head as disappointed as the night of, but the smile she wears on this night warms my heart.

"I begged you to apologize to that bitch, and as much as you didn't want to, as much as the mafia Italian in you didn't want to apologize, you did."

She closes her eyes, nodding her head, remembering the night distinctly. Illegra can feel that love I had for her; closing her eyes puts her back in my shoes that night.

"That was the moment I knew I loved you. That was the moment I realized that I wanted you in my life. Not because you apologized, but because you didn't want to apologize but still did; you did that for me."

I pause, and our world stills. Something in the air is more potent than nostalgia or recollection, something more important than past transgressions or future hopes.

"Something about that changed me; it was the first time I was proud to be with someone."

I hear the old man in my ear talking about the price that no young man wants to pay, talking about the prize that I will get. The price admits that you can not live without her, acknowledging that my life would be nothing without her.

"Tonight, I met myself 50 years from now, a man without you..."

Illegra looks at me with the sapphire of confusion; she tries hard to understand but can't.

"...and I didn't like what I saw. I know it makes no sense, but just listen."

I scoot closer to her, grab both of her hands, then hold them, grasping them like never before. My fingertips were in the palms of her hands while my thumbs caressed her silky, alabaster skin. I hear the old man one last time in my head, and my onyx begins to leak.

"You will realize the one price you should have paid was the easiest price to pay."

Those words echo as I hold Illegra's hands close to my face. I'm shaking with excitement, trembling with fear, then the words fall out.

"I love you."

Illegra looks at me speechless, perplexed by the goings-on. It is the first time I have ever formed these words, but they come out so effortlessly that they still seem to shock the entire universe.

"Fuck the relationship status, fuck my boys, fuck all of this… I want to spend the rest of my life with you.."

I release Illegra's hands and get up off the bed in excitement, nervously pacing back and forth on her end. Finally, I get down on one knee and then again grab her hands. Face flushed with excitement—heated from a slight embarrassment, but she is also puzzled by this vibrant confusion.

"Illegra Tiffany Russo, I know I have been an ass, I know this past year has been hell, but will you do me the honors of making me the luckiest man on the planet; will you become my wife?"

She looks down at me, opens her mouth, and first says.

"Are you asking me what I think you are?"

I nod yes, more emotional than ever before, as the onyx continues to drip, leaking every feeling I have hidden over the years. Those beautiful sapphire eyes become filled with such emotion that I am confused and unsure what that look holds. There is a long pause, a shared pause that is both terrifying and needed. The whole world is still while she looks down at our hands together, then looks into the onyx.

"I…"

What sort of elixir develops in her eyes? Is it happiness? Is it sadness? Are these tears of joy, or are they tears of the final conclusion after so many would-be break-ups? I begin feeling suffocated by inpatients and fearful of what comes next. One minute feels like an hour, and this hot room might just be the master bedroom from hell.

"I-I don't know what to say."

Illegra's fumble of words makes me vibrate, the whole room shakes, and I grab her hands. I grab her hands with no intention of letting go, grasping them like never before, holding her as though she were my only grip on this mad world.

The old man spoke of a price, a priceless price that no man wants to pay, and that price is love; it is the key. No young man wants to pay the fee of the heart, the highest cost, the most invaluable of currency.

I look into sapphire blue eyes with all of the sparks, all of the fire, all of the electricity of our love, and the millions of loves from all of time. Every love story and song, every poem, with the onyx of devotion, I look into Illegra, ready to reconcile from this night and commit like no young buck is willing to commit.

"I love you and only you. I want you to be my wife."

"Malic I…"

Holding her hands, feeling the warmth of her flesh, seeing the electricity of onyx connected to sapphire, and sapphire connected back to my deep dark onyx colored eyes, eyes that have seen the past, the future, eyes that now live in the present, bearing witness to Illegra's beautiful lips as they form the phrase, "I do."

Finally, I know with all my heart that this is not the end, for at this moment, right here, right now, the two of us, filled with water in our eyes balling like a couple of romantics, I know that this could not be the end; it is only the beginning.

The End

(The end is the beginning is, the end is the beginning)

Epilogue:

If you are reading this, you have purchased and finished the raw, unedited release of "The Old Man and the Sazerac," and for that, I thank you. I specifically released this story the way it is without the help of any editors or too many eyes for a few reasons. First, since the age of seven, as a person who has wanted nothing more than to write books and be published, I feel it is my right of passage to take this honest journey for my first book. Regardless of the outcome, the success or failure, one thing will remain steadfast and faithful, I wrote and completed a book on my own. With little to no educational guidance. My second reason for laying out this version happens to be the dark circumstances in which this book was created; the battles I went through, the people who kept me alive, and the state of my fragile mind. "The Old Man and the Sazerac is a book written in perhaps that darkest time of my life, but before I divulge these dark moments of my existence, let me once again thank you for not only reading "The Old Man and the Sazerac," but for joining me on this journey into a writing career forty years in the making. I was created to write stories, and hopefully, you will keep reading them.

I am a Writer: How this book came to be.

The year was 2019, a year that I will soon be writing "Black Heart, Dark Mind," my second novel coming next year. Here you will only get the cliff notes of what led me to the story "The Old Man and the Sazerac." After being arrested on a cruise ship in Key West, Fl, charged with two felonies, fired from my management job in Harlem, hustled out of a twelve thousand dollar business deal, and then homeless in Miami, I felt my life was over. All of this happened before March. Feeling destitute of life, love, and purpose, I began posting my complete mental breakdown on social media, which caught the attention of many friends, but only one reached an immediate solution. Erica J. Harvey convinced me that one option was for me to leave Miami behind and head home to Las Vegas. At this moment, I felt saved and said yes, but first, Erica said we would make a detour.

After three days in the nastiest hostel in all of Florida, Erica flew me to L.A., where I would join her at Tony Robbins UPW(Unleash The Power

Within) Conference. I will spare you all of the details of the Conference, all of the details of my mental state when dealing with thousands of screaming, positive people. Instead, I will be honest. When I was in Miami, I was barback, homeless, and all I could do was drink. I was drinking and drinking; I had drunk so much that by the time I was in the presence of Erica, I was an alcoholic, almost entirely dependent on the liquid of my demise. Admittedly I was not so much drinking as much as I wanted to kill myself. I wanted to end it but did not have the means to accomplish it or the balls. Thinking back at my state, I should have never taken Erica's offer. I was so broke, broken, and suicidal, and she had a teenage son living with her. Nevertheless, with death as my backpack, I flew to L.A. and participated with a smile on my face. Throughout this time, thoughts of suicide lived in the back behind my eyelids during UPW and my entire time in Las Vegas.

I was defeated, feeling beat by a system I thought I had figured out, and crushed that I had finally become those stereotypes I spent my whole life running from. Ten hours in a Key West jail robbed me of so much, and my dignity was utterly shattered. Living my life as whitewashed as I did was a tactic, this defense mechanism created to help me get jobs and into doors that other brothas and sistas couldn't. I took great pride in my skillful diction and how so many thought I dressed like a "white boy," yet when I was arrested—when I was charged with those two felonies, then that farce of privilege disappeared, and I was just another Black face. This was the realization I was coming to feel, that darkness I had been running from my entire life, and perhaps I deserved that outcome? Maybe I needed to wake up? And even though at UPW, I hadn't been charged with felons quite yet, within my mind already knew. Once I was arrested, my whole being knew, and it felt so close to the end, and if it wasn't the end, I sure felt like ending it before cuffs would ever be placed on me again. Fortunately, those crazy positive people at UPW gave me a few sparks here and there, and Erica for being as supportive as she was; otherwise, those dark moments could have turned into tragedy. I would be remiss if I did not acknowledge the power and positive influence UPW has. Sure some of the activities are campy, some of the people are so in your face positive that you begin doubting yourself, but overall I came away from UPW with a, let's say, different outlook.

At UPW, we screamed, cried, and took loads of notes. It was amazing being in this building with thousands considering a week before Toni Robbins was on this jumbotron talking, I was walking the streets of South Beach drunk and homeless; one night, I was so drunk that I didn't wake up in a random house or even a random bush, I woke up walking. You read that right; I woke up, and I was walking the streets of Miami close to a Coliseum with no way of knowing how I got there or where my phone was. And then I was at UPW talking about changing the world. It was incredible, the people were fantastic, but nothing could quiet my thoughts of suicide.

The way I viewed it, my life was over, and this UPW was the one last hoorah before taking my life in Vegas, like a sign that I could go. It was a very morbid time in my life when this black boulder of calamity just seemed to demolish everything. Still, before that boulder completely crushed me, I listened to Tony Robbins and Joseph Mclendon III. I watched as these two men inspired thousands. In all fairness, I was not buying all of what they were "selling," and most of the Conference seemed to be a commercial for some other conference. But I did respect what was going on. I began to understand not what Toni Robbins was selling but what he was able to accomplish. Eventually, I concluded that my best course of action was to write a book before ending it all.

When Erica and I arrived back in Vegas, I spent three weeks on her couch just writing. My goal was to see if I could do it, to see if I could write before I gave it all up. I had a few stipulations before I wrote. First and foremost, it could not be a story about or from my life or my current situation. Second, the story had to be made up entirely, landscape, characters, and all. And lastly, Braxton, Erica's son, had to be a character. In my mind, it was a way to prove to myself that this was a story pulled from virtually nowhere. Oddly enough, I took

to this challenge like a fish to water (I apologize in advance to Erica and

Braxton because they will assuredly be asked about this moment.), writing more

than speaking. WritingRegistering more than I ate. On that couch, with

headphones on that Erica was kind enough to give me with headphones on that

Erica was kind enough to give me on that couch, I found myself on the blank

page. Zone out, I had not one suicidal thought as I was pleasantly trapped, lulled

by words that seemed to fall from my mind onto the page. It was enthralling,

and even though I only had an Ipad to write on, I made it work.

Three weeks later, and not a drop of alcohol, I finished my first novel. It

was exciting that I was finally doing what I loved no matter the circumstance,

and for a moment, I basked in that feeling, almost alive again. Unfortunately,

time can be cruel to a defeated mind, and falling into old routines creates the

most diabolical obstacles for a lost soul. As I began working in the service

industry of Las Vegas again came back to that dark passenger of suicidal

thoughts and drinking in excess. Rightfully fearing the damage my state might

create around her son, Erica politely asked me to leave, and I obliged. After that,

life becomes a blur of alcohol, attempted suicide, and 96 hours in Las Vegas,

Psyche-Ward, and eventually moving back to Texas.

Throughout this time, "The Old Man and the Sazerac" lay wasted in the "cloud," doomed never to be read. I remember laying in that hospital bed with only my thoughts--with only those so many regrets. So broken, I was more than broken; I was utterly destroyed, lost, and all I could think while lying in that hospital bed was how it was that I had never published a book. I laid in that bed realizing that I hadn't failed because I got fired in New York, I hadn't failed because I had now become an alcoholic, I hadn't failed because I wasn't working at the number 1 club or restaurant, and I hadn't even failed because I was now a two-time felon. No, those were not my failures; those were just wrong turns, unforced errors of a lost life. But where I failed myself, my life was not listening to that voice in my head telling me to write. For most, those voices in their head lead them astray, causing mental insecurity and complications, yet some of us need to listen to that voice. I was not the writer I know I am. Laying in that hospital bed, I learned that the only way I could ever hope to save myself was through my devotion to the blank page, listening to that voice within, and allowing that voice a place to speak.

There are so many people that I must thank for being here alive, but one of the most critical factors that kept me busy is my love for the blank page and the words I write. At its core, "The Old Man and the Sazerac" is a story about finding oneself regardless of what is popular or cool. Irrespective of how much money you make. And oddly enough, I believe this was a message that I was trying to write to an Ebony man who had given up on the world and love. I am so glad that I did not give up. I am so thankful that I have decided to write instead.

Acknowledgments:

With so many people who have emotionally and even financially contributed to my life these recent years, I must first begin by thanking Rob & Rod. I cannot recall much of the day I would take my life. I remember the cops at the door, the handcuffs, and 96 hours in a psych-ward. Laying in that hospital bed, I was thinking of books, suicide, and wondering whom the fuck called the suicide hotline. Initially, I believed that it was a dear friend and ex-lover who had called. I was so mad at her, and for that, Azreal, I apologize and will apologize again and again. I am sorry. When I was eventually released, and someone got back to my phone, I soon found out that it was Rob & Rod who had decided after careful deliberation that calling the suicide hotline would be best.

When I found this out, I was initially disappointed, feeling that they might not understand my plight; I couldn't have been more wrong. From my arrest in Florida, all of the way up until now have; I say this regretfully, but these two men have financially supported me when no one would give a felon a job. They have both been like mentors to me over our friendship, providing insight, reading excerpts of my work, and often suggesting some of the most excellent mentals practices to help nurture a fractured mind. These two men, Rod Grozier

& Robert Garret Smith, had faith in me when I had lost all faith in everything, and for that, I would like to sincerely send all of my love and extreme thanks to these two remarkable men.

I would also love to thank…

Erica J. Harvey, thank you for being a friend even after my debacle. Erica, you have always been there for me, and I will never forget our times together. Thank you for taking me in and allowing me a great space to write. Also, let Brax know that he will be a Star someday; big "S."

Michelle Arbeau, thank you for taking a chance when literally no other publisher or agent would. Your energy and positive words have put this troubled mind at ease. I look forward to a long and mutually rewarding relationship filled with more stories and new risks. Thank you for helping me make my dream a reality.

To Kisha, Ron, Dee, Mom, and the entire Laneaux family, thank you for reminding me that although I may not be blood, I will always be family. Thank you for being a mom to me when I forgot what that meant. Ron, thank you for being a brother and my lifeline during the pandemic.

And to Mak, I did it. I finally wrote you that book you've been asking for; thank you, Makaila. Love you, sis.